Phantom and the Fugitive

by

Gail MacMillan

This is a work of fiction. Names, characters, places, and incidents are either the product of the author's imagination or are used fictitiously, and any resemblance to actual persons living or dead, business establishments, events, or locales, is entirely coincidental.

Phantom and the Fugitive

COPYRIGHT © 2015 by Gail MacMillan

Cover Art by *Debbie Taylor*

The Wild Rose Press, Inc.
PO Box 708
Adams Basin, NY 14410-0708
Visit us at www.thewildrosepress.com

Publishing History
First Crimson Rose Edition, 2015
Print ISBN 978-1-5092-0290-4
Digital ISBN 978-1-5092-0291-1

Published in the United States of America

"The girl! Where is she?"

Something that sounded like a curse in a foreign language followed. She listened to footsteps pounding about the cottage, at one point directly over her head. Finally they stopped.

"This is not a time to go rushing madly about," the second foreign voice commented. "She can't get off this island. We'll find her. Make sure Rockenfeller does as instructed. I want that spy in the farmhouse burned to ashes."

"Of course."

"I'll come with you. We'll look for the girl along the way. She must have gotten outside."

Hurried footsteps marked a departure. Danielle swallowed hard and drew a deep breath. She could do it. She had to. No matter how Andrew—Andy—Drack had deceived her, she couldn't allow him to be murdered.

She waited for what seemed an eternity. At last, convinced by the silence above that the cottage was deserted, she decided to make her move.

Shaking so violently she could barely coordinate her movements, she eased the hatch open a crack and surveyed the kitchen. Empty. She crept up the steps and out onto the kitchen floor.

Drawing a deep breath, she bolted to her feet and sprinted out the back door into the darkness and the long, dead grass behind the cottage. *I have to warn Andy. I have to.* The words chanted inside her head as she ran toward the cover of the forest of black spruce.

"There she goes! Stop her!"

Dedication

To Bibsy and Bruiser, friends and companions

Chapter One

Fugitive. I'm a fugitive. Me. Danielle Burgess.

Glancing into her rearview mirror to check for police pursuit, she couldn't believe it. Only last Friday she'd been an archivist at the Eastern Coast Museum in Halifax, Nova Scotia, thrilled at the anticipation of going to Montreal for a romantic weekend with super sexy, charismatic, Doctor of Archeology Harry Stone.

With an effort she shoved away thoughts of the handsome doctor and forced her mind back to her present situation. Would the police find her here in this remote corner of northeastern New Brunswick? Would they even bother to search for her in Atlantic Canada? Given the magnitude of her crime, would they assume she'd head for some foreign locale?

Harry had advised her present destination would be safest.

"It's an old cottage my great-aunt left me," he said. "I've put it up for rent through an agency, but so far, no takers. That's probably because it's on a deserted island off the coast of New Brunswick. Hasn't been used since she died last spring, but there's an old fellow, a former friend of Aunt Hester, who's seen to its care. His name is Jimmy Waters. He'll ferry you out to the island. I'll make the arrangements. You'll be safe there until I can come for you."

"Harry…"

"Listen to me, babe." He took her by the shoulders and gazed down into her eyes. "At the moment, all the evidence points right at you. Aside from Dr. Gervais Harrison—and he was in the hospital suffering from a heart attack at the time of the robbery—you were the only one with the security code to the museum, the only one who had access to those artifacts. With no signs of a break-in, the Royal Canadian Mounted Police are all too ready to lock you up and close the books on the case."

"But, Harry…"

"Please, just do as I say." He planted a kiss on her forehead. "Be a good girl, get into that clunker of a car, and head for Phantom Island. If anyone asks, you're a photographer out to get shots of the Fire Ship ghost the area is famous for. I've thrown a bunch of my own photography equipment in the back seat. And here…" He pulled a thick roll of bills from his pocket and thrust them into her hand. "This should be enough to cover your needs until I can get this mess cleaned up. Don't use any plastic."

"All right." Still in shock, she took the money without really being aware of what she was doing.

"The nearest settlement on the mainland is a place called Cavalier's Cove." He released her and turned to run his hand over the nondescript gray car he'd purchased for her at a pre-owned vehicle lot near the Quebec/New Brunswick border. "Since the local fish processing plant closed, the village has become little more than a ghost town, the far end of nowhere. Stay on the island until I contact you. Under no circumstances try to get in touch with me. Because of our relationship, they'll probably put a trace on my calls."

She'd done as he instructed, watching him with glances in her rearview mirror until a bend in the road took him from her sight.

****

The moment Danielle Burgess saw the former little fishing community of Cavalier's Cove, she knew Harry hadn't exaggerated his description. He could have added a footnote about its ambience of utter desolation and still remained well within the realm of truth. Huddled beside the pot-holed secondary road that followed coastal ins and outs like a disgruntled snake, the little cluster of buildings appeared to have lain vulnerable to the caprices of marine elements for decades.

Cavalier's Cove consisted of a dozen weatherbeaten, gray, shingled houses, a small church surrounded by canted, moss-encrusted grave markers, and a false-fronted general store, the few shards of paint remaining suggesting it had once been dark red in color. A pair of vintage gas pumps stood in front.

Further along the road that served as the village's only street, she recognized the sharply pitched roof and long, narrow windows of an old-fashioned, single-roomed schoolhouse. Boarded up, its yard overgrown with tall, scraggly weeds, it bore bitter testimony to a lack of faith in any resurgence of population.

Beyond the church and store, a lane cut off from the road and led to a crumbling wharf. There, a wooden barge with a rusted tugboat attached occupied a ferry slip. Beside it floated a lobster boat, its white paint so tattered it appeared more derelict than seaworthy as it sat moored in the deadly still water. Not a single human being was in sight.

Probably this cold day is keeping the residents indoors. It is late October in northern New Brunswick, after all. Cavalier's Cove can't actually be a ghost town.

With a sick, sinking feeling invading body and soul, she shifted back into drive. As she passed the general store, she saw it. Her breath caught in her throat. Hidden behind the abandoned schoolhouse a small white building, the only freshly painted one in the village, held a sign that declared it to be the "Cavalier's Cove Detachment of the Royal Canadian Mounted Police." Had Harry known the Mounties had a detachment in this Godforsaken place?

A tall man wearing the uniform of an RCMP officer emerged. He paused on the doorstep and glanced in her direction.

She pulled off the road and braked to a stop. Her hands broke out in cold sweat as they gripped the steering wheel, and her stomach knotted. Had he been informed she was in the vicinity?

After what seemed an eternity, the officer turned away, adjusted his hat, and proceeded down the steps to get into his cruiser. As he swung the vehicle around and headed in the opposite direction, she slumped against the steering wheel, weak with relief.

Idiot! She released the brake. *As if a policeman in this backwater would be looking for a fugitive from Halifax. Anyway, I won't be staying in Cavalier's Cove. I'll be out on Phantom Island.*

She snapped on her signal light and turned onto the dirt road leading to the wharf. As she eased along the lane, she scanned the bay for her new home.

It wasn't difficult to locate. The dark, ragged lump

of land sitting alone out on the flat, iron-gray water looked as inviting as Alcatraz in the fading light of the dreary late October afternoon. Scraggy trees bent by the prevailing winds stood scattered raggedly along its zenith. She couldn't see any buildings. They had to be on the far side, facing out toward the North Atlantic. Although the small island appeared far away, Danielle, a lifelong resident of seafront communities in Nova Scotia, knew how deceptive distances over water could be.

She stopped the car at the decrepit ferry ramp and got out. Where was this Jimmy Waters person who was supposed to take her out to that dismal place, who had supposedly been acting as caretaker of the cottage? Harry had contacted him yesterday, made the arrangements…hadn't he?

The thought had no sooner cleared her mind than a little man appeared out of the cabin of the tugboat. *Good Lord, a cross between a gnome and a leprechaun.* Barely five feet tall, he appeared as old and weathered as the buildings of Cavalier's Cove. In a ragged plaid mackinaw, faded overalls, and patched rubber boots, he had a weather-darkened face as wrinkled as a prune. In contrast, the sapphire-blue eyes that looked out at Danielle from beneath the peak of his water-stained baseball cap were bright and piercing.

"Ya must be the woman what wants ta go out ta Phantom Island ta try ta get a pitcher of the Fire Ship," he said, looking her over critically. "Well, it's good ya ain't lookin' fer anything else, 'cause there ain't much out there 'sides ghosts. Since the cannery closed, not even the herrin' gulls go there anymore."

"I'm Dani Breckenreid." Struggling to force aside

her misgivings, Danielle used her alias and extended her hand. "Yes, I'm a photographer, hoping to get a shot of your famous Fire Ship. I'll be staying at the Matthews cottage. You're Mr. Waters, I presume?"

"That's me." He took her hand in a strong, firm grip, surprising given his frail appearance. "Only I don't much like bein' called mister. Jimmy's the ticket. Are ya ready ta go? They're predictin' heavy fog fer tanight, and I'd like ta get back here 'fore it rolls in, while the water's still flat as a pancake."

"Of course. You mentioned ghosts. I thought the place was named Phantom Island because it's a vantage point for spotting the legendary Fire Ship…the ship doomed to forever roam the seas, its sails in flames because the captain had abducted a young bride."

"Well, sure, that's part of it." Jimmy Waters squinted up at her. "The main reason, though, is 'cause of the Horseman what rides the island's beaches."

"Horseman?"

"Legend has it he's the ghost of one of them there Cavalier fellas what stuck up fer King Charles a while back. When the King got hisself beheaded, this fella took his black horse and lit out for America on the next ship. The vessel got wrecked off the north end of Phantom Island in a big October storm. Him and his horse was the only survivors."

"Really? I haven't heard that story." *Just what I need. A ghostly horseman to keep me company. Hopefully he isn't headless.*

"They managed ta swim ta shore but died of exposure and exhaustion at the base of a cliff about a quarter mile above the cottage," the old man continued his tale. "Some fishermen found 'em there and buried 'em as best they could. Not long after, they started seein' a fella ridin' up and down the beach at night on a big black horse, his cape streamin' out in the wind, a wide-brimmed hat with a plume on his head. That's when they named the place Phantom Island...and this place Cavalier's Cove."

"Does this ghostly cavalier still haunt its beaches?" Danielle tried to sound casual. "Maybe I can get a photo of him."

"Naw!" Jimmy flapped his hand disparagingly. "He ain't been seen in over fifty years. Maybe he went back to England to help this here new Charles what's goin' ta be King someday." He squeaked out a chuckle. "Now get aboard. Don't look like much, but I guarantee it'll hold yer vehicle. Used to carry some good-sized trucks when the cannery was open and this place was home to a big fleet of fishin' boats."

"What happened?" Danielle indicated the rotting wharf.

"Big, new, modern fish-processing plant opened thirty miles down shore. Little operation like the one on Phantom Island couldn't compete. Folks and boats had to move away. It's as simple as that." He paused and heaved a deep sigh. "Now all that's left is a bunch of us old folks...and the Mountie." He jerked a finger toward the small white building.

"I suppose it comes under the heading of progress." Danielle directed the conversation away from Cavalier's Cove's lawman. "I appreciate your coming out to ferry me to Phantom Island, Mr. Waters. It's a cold day." She rubbed her hands together and wished she had gloves.

"I took Hettie and her cat out there in April, soon

as the ice was out of the bay," he said, pausing to look out over the water. "She was right possessed with the idea of capturin' a spook with that camera of hers this year. Guess she figured time was runnin' out. She was pushin' ninety. She must have overdone it. Only two weeks later, I get an SOS from the Mountie for me to go out and check on Hettie. She hadn't finished a transmission to him, and he was worried.

"I took off right fast and found her lying on the floor by that there CB radio. Even when she was gasping for breath while I was bringing her off the island that last time, she kept repeatin' something about a pitcher of a ghost ridin' a big black horse. I reckon she was out of her head, poor soul."

"Maybe I'll have better luck," she replied. "I understand late October is the time it most commonly puts in an appearance." Some of the information Harry had given her while he was packing her off came back to her.

"Yeah, if it ever does." Jimmy Waters scratched his head under his battered cap. "It ain't on any schedule, ya know. People has come here and waited and waited and waited fer nothin'. What'd you say was the name of the fella who you rented the cottage from?" He squinted up at her, sapphire eyes narrowing.

"I rented it through an agency."

"Ah, yeah, right. Now it all makes sense. Yesterday I got a call from a fella saying he was with Island Rentals. He informed me that you was comin' and to make sure you got out to the cottage, seein' as how I'm the caretaker. Seemed a bit strange at the time, since I recall Hettie tellin' me she was leavin' the place to a relative workin' in Egypt…her great nephew, some kind of archeologist fella. He must have put it up fer rent. Think he'll ever show up out here?"

"I shouldn't think so. Otherwise he wouldn't have had the agency list the cottage for rent. Now about the Fire Ship…"

"Odds are agen seein' it, ya know."

"I'll take my chances." Danielle struggled to exude a confidence she was far from feeling.

"Suit yourself, but don't count on gettin' any help spottin' it from that fella who lives in the farmhouse. He's blind as a bat."

"Someone is already living on the island? There's a farm? I thought the cottage was the only structure on it."

"There's a deserted fish plant and a farm out there, too. No one's lived in the farmhouse for years. Then this young lad shows up in May, shortly after Hettie passed, and rents it." Jimmy Waters' tone softened, and he shook his head sadly. "Lost his sight in a bad car crash, poor young fella. Still limps a bit, too. Good-lookin' young man, I'd guess, behind those dark glasses he seems dead set on wearin' day and night."

"Why would a blind man choose to live alone on a deserted island?" Danielle's astonishment reflected in her tone.

"Beats me." The old man shrugged. "His buddy is the constable at the RCMP detachment in the village. He coulda gone ta live with him, but, no, he was bound and determined ta move out there alone." He swung an arm to indicate the island. "Him and his wolf."

"Wolf!" *The plot of this real-life nightmare is thickening way too fast.*

"Well, he claims it's a dog, but I never saw no dog

with eyes like that…pure gold, probably glow in the dark."

"Does this blind hermit have a name?"

"Yeah. Andrew Drack, pronounced like in Dracula…you know, the Count." He chuckled wickedly.

"Who brings his supplies?"

"I ferry Constable James out with groceries and the like once a week. By the by, if you want ta get in touch with me ta ferry ya back ta the mainland or anything else ya might need, ya'll have ta call the Mountie on the CB ya'll find in the cottage. He'll get in touch with me, and I'll come, weather permittin'. There's no telephone lines out there, and they tell me them newfangled cellular ones don't work on the island. Maybe the Phantom messes up the transmissions." His blue eyes twinkled maliciously.

"There's no other way?" The thought of contacting the RCMP made Danielle's stomach lurch.

"Not unless ya got homin' pigeons on ya." Again the squeaky chuckle. "Now, we'd better get started fer the island. That fog bank off to the nor'east looks like its headin' this way pretty quick. Drive your car onto the ferry slow and easy while I crank up the engine."

He limped out along the ferry slip and across the barge to the rusted little tugboat. With a grunt, he dropped down onto the deck.

Danielle paused to assess the barge's makeshift vehicle ramp. It made the approaches Evel Knievel used for his death-defying stunts look like cakewalks.

"Are ya comin'?" Jimmy Waters stuck his head out of the cabin as smoke from the diesel engine belched from the boat's rusting stack.

"Right away," she replied and climbed back into her car. Shifting into drive, she eased the old car down the ramp.

Her hands clamped the steering wheel like vises, but she made it.

"All aboard," Jimmy Waters yelled.

The engine coughed to life, smoke billowed from the stack, and the old vessel started off. As the improvised ferry chugged out into the bay, Danielle pulled on the emergency brake and got out of her vehicle. She'd have a better chance of survival outside her car if the contraption decided to sink. As always, the thought of being trapped broke her out in a cold sweat.

She shivered and turned up her collar against a chill half physical, half emotional. The more-fashionable-than-warm faux-suede jacket she wore over a turtleneck above designer jeans she'd purchased at an outrageous price for her weekend with Harry did little to ward off the damp cold. Thank heavens she'd had the good sense to wear running shoes instead of those sexy stiletto-heeled sandals she'd purchased especially for her now aborted romantic weekend.

She wrapped her arms across the front of her body and rubbed her forearms. This couldn't be happening. Any second now she'd wake up and find herself back in her nice safe cubicle at the museum, busily cataloguing artifacts, with dear old Dr. Gervais Harrison peering nearsightedly over her shoulder at her work. The doctor, in his shabby cardigans and baggy trousers, gray hair desperately in need of a good barber, personified the term absent-minded professor. Anything aside from what involved his work he promptly forgot. In the three months since he'd come to work at the museum, she'd even had to remind him when it was lunch or closing time.

And then Harry Stone had arrived.

When the doctor stepped off Egyptian Airlines Flight 243 three weeks earlier at the Halifax International Airport, she'd done a double-take. With hair the color she believed might be similar to that of desert sands and eyes that reminded her of rich milk chocolate, the man sported a six-foot tall body that just wouldn't quit and a face that personified the term ruggedly handsome.

Indiana Jones, move over! This is a real-life hero. Thank you, Dr. Harrison, for assigning me the task of welcoming him to Nova Scotia.

Meeting him had done nothing to lower that opinion. He had a grin that creased his sun-bronzed face in all the right places and a laidback manner that exuded an earthy virility. No slouch in personality, either, he emanated warmth and sincerity coupled with a charismatic charm and ready sense of humor designed to sweep a woman off her feet.

When he asked her to dinner that evening and most of the following evenings, she never once refused. Archivist Danielle Burgess believed she was falling in love...if she wasn't already there.

She'd envisioned Harry taking her back to Egypt as his partner on his next expedition, sharing blockbuster-movie-type adventures...nothing like this sordid horror. Not running from the law, the prime suspect in a theft of Egyptian antiquities worth millions, threatened with incarceration. Given her acute claustrophobia, imprisonment would be hell on earth.

She wondered what Harry was doing at this moment. He'd arrived in Halifax a day after a magnificent collection of Egyptian artifacts from the Cairo Museum had been delivered to her place of employment. He had been commissioned to accompany it, but a bout of illness had delayed him by twenty-four hours.

Dating Harry Stone and listening to his amazing tales of adventure had kept her enthralled by both the stories and the man. Then everything had changed. She cringed as her thoughts went back to that awful moment when she'd been sitting in the passenger seat of Harry Stone's rented sports car on their way to a romantic weekend in Montreal.

Harry had paused to gas up, and Danielle had taken advantage of the break in their journey to head into the service station's washroom to use the facility and repair her makeup. Thinking how movie-star-handsome Harry was, she'd looked over at him as she got back into the vehicle.

Wow! And I'm off for the weekend with the man. Danielle Burgess, your life has definitely taken a turn into the fast lane, a long way from cataloguing dusty bits and pieces in a grungy museum basement week in and week out.

He stopped for traffic before moving back out onto the TransCanada Highway, and flashed her one of his sexy grins. As he swung out onto the road a moment later, he punched a change on the car radio. A soft, romantic ballad wafted around them.

Am I falling in love? I must be. This is the wildest thing I've ever done, taking off with a man I've known barely a month.

Then it happened. She still found it difficult to believe her life had been shattered by something as simple as a change from music to a news broadcast.

"This just in," the professionally cool voice announced. "Danielle Burgess, archivist at the Eastern Coast Museum in Halifax, is being sought in connection with a multi-million-dollar theft of Egyptian artifacts from that facility. The collection had been on loan from the Cairo Museum. Burgess was one of only two people who had security access to the priceless artifacts. The other individual, Dr. Gervais Harrison, was admitted to hospital late last week with a suspected heart attack and has yet to be released. With no signs of forced entry, RCMP are searching for Burgess as a person of interest."

"Harry! What…they can't possibly think…! This is insane!"

She only vaguely remembered Harry snapping off the radio, pulling the car to a stop on the shoulder of the road, and taking her into his arms.

Later, when she got over the initial shock, she found a miniscule degree of comfort in the fact that her parents and brother were out of the country and would probably not hear of the accusations for at least a day or two, maybe not until they returned to this country. She squeezed her eyes shut and prayed.

Please, please don't let the story be sufficiently important to attract international interest. There must be enough wars and murders to keep journalists busy on other events.

****

She brought herself back to the moment and present conditions. How long could she exist on this forlorn-looking scrap of an island, with a blind man and his wolf as her only neighbors? She considered the idea of telling the old man to turn his clumsy vessel around and take her back to the mainland. It would be simple. She'd turn herself in to that policeman and end it all.

The moment passed as quickly as it had come, as Harry Stone's voice echoed back to her, detailing the evidence against her and the possibility of a lengthy jail sentence. Running her hand through the short dark curls of her freshly cut hair, she sighed. She'd always been proud of her long, golden-brown hair even though her job had required she wear it up or tied back. Allowing Harry to crop it off and buy her a hair dye kit would never have been an option in any other circumstance. Darkening her face with a heavy application of tanning lotion had completed her transformation from Danielle Burgess, archivist, to Dani Breckenreid, photographer of the paranormal.

Harry had done all he could for her, she thought, remembering the thick roll of bills he'd thrust into her hand on their parting and her amazement when she'd stopped to buy supplies and discovered just how much cash he'd given her. Just how long did he expect it to be before he could come for her, that he thought she'd need so much money?

She looked off across the water. The fog Jimmy Waters had mentioned was moving in from the sea, its gray curtain pushing a wave of bone-chilling air in front of it. It slithered around her and started her teeth chattering. Still, she could not bring herself to get back in the car. The vision of drowning, trapped inside the vehicle as the old vessel sank beneath the dark surface of the water, was enough to keep her enduring the cold on deck.

"I'll have ta head back as soon as ya get off." The old man stuck his head out of the tug's cabin and yelled at her above the throb of the engine. "Can't risk gettin' caught out here in that stuff." He indicated the thickening mist. "But before I do, I'll give ya the key and instructions on gettin' ta the cottage."

Five minutes later, she eased the old car off the rickety craft and into two wheel tracks leading from the crude ferry landing. The trail crossed hard beach sand before winding its way into waist-high, frost-killed marsh grass and toward a shadowy forest of scraggly black spruce. She stopped the car, got out, and returned to where Jimmy waited on the barge's deck.

"Here's the key ta the cottage." He handed her a keyring with a design of a sailing ship in flames. "Hettie's key. The lights, heat, and water are all set up. I saw ta that yesterday when I got the call someone was comin' ta live there."

Harry, pretending to be a rental agent, had done a good job. She'd stood beside him in a small motel near the New Brunswick-Quebec border while he made the call.

"All ya have ta do is fuel the generator in the shed behind the cottage every day or so," the old man was continuing. "I left instructions on how ta do that on the kitchen table. They're easy ta follow. Hettie did it, so I reckon a youngster like ya won't have any trouble."

"Thanks. How much do I owe you, Mr. Waters?" She reached for her purse.

"Ah!" He brushed the idea aside with a wave of a gnarled hand. "I did it for Hettie fer nothin' fer years. Reckon I won't start chargin' folks now. Just don't call me Mr. Waters no more, and we'll call it square."

His face crinkled into a grin that made Danielle smile back.

"That's generous of you, Jimmy. Now if you'll direct me to the cottage, I'll let you get back to the mainland."

"Sure, sure. Just follow them tracks back into the trees fer about a quarter mile. The road branches three ways there. The one on the left will take ya right ta the cottage."

"And the other two?"

"The overgrown one on the right leads ta the old cannery. The middle one"—Jimmy squinted at her— "takes ya ta the farmhouse on the cliff where Andrew Drack and his wolf live."

"So they're my next-door neighbors."

"Well, yeah, I reckon. His place is about a quarter mile down the beach from the cottage, so I never thought of it like that." Jimmy looked back over the water. "That fog's movin' in fast. I'll be goin'. Call the Mountie if ya need anything, and I'll come out directly, weather permittin'."

He turned and limped back onto his ferry. With a grunt, he dropped down onto the deck of the tug and vanished into the cabin. Danielle watched as he fired up the engine, with a belching of smoke, and backed the awkward barge out into the water. When he'd succeeded in turning it toward the mainland, she waved farewell, climbed back into her car, and started the motor.

She looked at the wheel tracks leading through the brown grass and into the darkening depth of the trees. Evening was descending over the island in long, ominous shadows. Nerve-rattling fear skittered over her. For two cents she'd jump out of that car and hail Jimmy to return for her.

She quelled the impulse as fast as it arrived. It would be absolutely the worst thing she could do. She'd just have to start considering this entire fiasco an adventure, something to tell her grandchildren…if she survived to have any.

Setting her lips in a hard, determined line, she shifted into drive and headed across the beach, through the grass, and into the forest. Five-thirty already. She glanced at the dashboard clock. She'd have to hurry if she wanted to get settled into the cottage before October's early evening darkness and the approaching fog overwhelmed the place.

As she entered the trees, she turned her headlights on high beam and pressed harder on the accelerator. Bumping over roots and ruts, she drove the quarter mile to the fork in the road. She was about to swing to the left when something silver flashed out of the darkness through the arc of her lights.

Her foot slammed down on the brakes. The car jolted to a stop. From the safety of roadside bushes, the animal paused and swung back to stare at her with glowing yellow eyes.

Andrew Drack's wolf! Good God, does the man let the brute roam free?

A tap on the window of her passenger door made her start so violently she lunged against her seatbelt. Swinging to her right, she saw a man's head and broad-shouldered upper torso in silhouette bending down to it.

Panic congealed into a suffocating blob at the back of her throat. Trapped. The man and his wolf had her at their mercy in the fog and encroaching darkness.

The outline spoke. "Good evening. I'm Andrew Drack."

Okay, okay. Calm down. You've got to face up to the situation. There's no way out.

Mustering what courage she could, Danielle leaned across the seat and cracked the window a couple of inches.

He's an accident victim, blind and lame, no one you can't handle.

"Good evening." She fought to keep shakiness out of her voice as she became aware of the dark glasses covering his eyes. "I'm"—she stumbled over the lie— "Dani Breckenreid. I've rented the cottage."

A smile crossed his lips, a slow, strangely sensuous smile. Something wafted over her, something that enveloped her with the intensity of an erotic moment.

What...!

She struggled back to reality.

He spoke again. "We're to be neighbors. I live in the farmhouse further up the shore."

"Sorry if I'll be disturbing your solitude." *Time to sound bold and confident, Danielle.* "I promise to stay out of your way. I'm a photographer, here to get a shot of the Fire Ship, not socialize."

She indicated the back seat with the camera equipment Harry had supplied to support her assumed profession, then flushed.

Smart move, Danielle, pointing them out to a blind man.

"Good luck. That's proven to be an elusive goal." He paused a moment, then continued, "Do you need help getting settled? Aladdin—that's my dog—and I have nothing but time." Bitterness tainted his last sentence.

Danielle paused. She'd scrutinized him more closely as her terror ebbed and discovered that he was early thirtyish and, from what she could see in the encroaching twilight and around the dark glasses, no slouch in the looks department.

"I'll be okay. Would you like a drive back to the farm? There's a cold fog drifting in, and it's getting…" *What am I doing. I don't know this man…and he's sending off these strange vibes…*

"Dark?" he finished. "I know. I can still distinguish night and day."

"I'm sorry. Of course, there must be various degrees of being visually challenged…"

"The word is blind. I hate euphemisms." The words snapped out.

"I'm sorry. Again."

"Well, don't be." His tone softened. "I'm the one who should apologize. I'd be grateful for a drive back to the farm. I left Aladdin's harness at the house and came out for a walk with only my cane. I'm tired of feeling my way. Is it okay if he gets a ride, as well?"

"He'll have to sit in back with the groceries and camera equipment." Remembering the supplies she'd purchased at a convenience store fifty miles away, Danielle released her seatbelt and leaned over to unlock the passenger door.

"He won't mind." Andrew Drack straightened up and whistled to the dog. "Come on, boy, this lady is picking us up. Hustle."

The big silver animal Danielle had glimpsed earlier bounded into the light that flashed on as his master opened the car's passenger door. Glancing over at Andrew Drack in the illumination, she suppressed an audible expletive.

He was one of the handsomest men she'd ever encountered—black curling hair, a face that would make any movie star envious, and a body in jeans, white T-shirt that clung to a broad chest, and black leather jacket that came straight out of her wildest fantasies. The only detriment to his appearance was those dark glasses, so black she could see nothing through them. But even they added to the ambience of sexy mysteriousness he exuded.

Stop it. Just stop it. It's simply this place and my weird situation. I'm not living in some quirky old-fashioned gothic novel...and this guy definitely isn't any Mr. Rochester.

She struggled to put her thoughts on pause as the dog leaped past his owner and vaulted into the back seat. There it circled until it had coiled its body into the small space remaining beside bags of groceries, several bottles of wine, and a collection of photographic equipment. Once seated, he settled his surreal stare on Danielle, tongue lolling over gleaming white fangs.

"You mentioned a harness. He's a seeing-eye dog?" Hoping she sounded a whole lot more cool and in control than she felt, she swung back to face forward.

"Among other things." He drew a white cane inside and collapsed it with a couple of quick snaps. "He's my companion, my eyes, my guardian, you name it. There's been just the two of us out here...until now."

The interior light winked out as he shut the door. Darkness enveloped them.

"What about your friend the RCMP officer?

Doesn't he visit regularly?"

"The Jimmy Waters grapevine must be as functional as ever." He chuckled. The sound, soft and sensual, sent a ripple of something she couldn't identify coursing through her. This man, coming out of the fog and darkness, sent visions of a gorgeous, mesmerizing vampire or warlock wafting across her mind.

Get back to reality, Danielle, and be quick about it!

"He does seem to know a lot about people and events in Cavalier's Cove," she replied, fighting her way out of her fantasies.

"Jimmy Waters is a good man to know if you need information on the area."

"Then the rental agency got me connected me with the right person."

"Rental agency?" He appeared only politely interested.

"Yes, that's how I found the cottage…when I was looking for a place to stay in the vicinity." She hoped her reply sounded equally casual.

"This rental company…they knew about Jimmy?" He used the same inflection again, but this time apprehension slowed her response.

Is he pursuing the subject or am I getting paranoid?

"Well, apparently he is the only source of transportation to the island. It made sense that they'd be aware of him and his service."

"I guess," he relieved her by replying casually. He paused before continuing, "I'd like you to reconsider my offer to help you settle in. It's pretty lonely out here. You might like some company, at least for a while."

"No, I'm sure…"

"Listen, Ms. Breckenreid, I thought moving to Phantom Island wouldn't be all that difficult." He turned to face her. "But it didn't take long for me to be grateful Wade James had insisted on accompanying me. Let me pass his kindness along by helping you."

"Well…" She hesitated.

"To still any misgivings you may have about me, I'll call Wade on the CB—I assume you have one in the cottage—and get him to vouch for my sterling character."

"No, really, that won't be necessary." The idea of his telling his RCMP friend about her presence caused her once again to break out in a cold sweat.

"I insist. I don't want you isolated on an island with someone you think you can't trust "

"When you put it like that, how can I refuse?" She struggled to make her words sound lighthearted and bantering, but a trapped feeling enveloped her as she shifted into drive and headed down the left trail as Jimmy Waters had instructed.

" 'Last night I dreamt I went to Manderley,' " she murmured the line from one of her favorite books as she proceeded down the overgrown trail.

"Must be gloomy and overgrown to inspire that quotation," he said as branches and weeds raked the sides and bottom of the car. "It's from du Maurier's *Rebecca*, the second Mrs. de Winter's words when she dreamed of returning to the mansion that had been a house of horrors for her, right?"

"You've read it?" She nearly drove into the trees as she took her attention from her driving to glance over at him in surprise. His knowledge of her favorite author astonished her. She'd never considered du Maurier male reading material.

"Yes, I've read all of her books. My favorite is *Frenchman's Creek*. I especially enjoyed her depiction of Dona's longing for romance and adventure. Have you read it?"

"Yes," she said.

"You probably enjoyed the Frenchman. What woman wouldn't be intrigued by a handsome outlaw who materializes nightly from the shadows to sweep a lady off her feet with his unbridled virility?" His tone softened, sending a strange thrill coursing through her.

Out of the tail of her eye she caught his expression and guessed he was either teasing or testing her. Maybe a little of both. She returned her attention to immediate concerns. The small car seemed enveloped in darkness, its headlights struggling to pierce the night. She and the enigmatic stranger were encased in an intimate world of their own.

"I hope the cottage is in better repair than this road." She struggled to bring her thoughts away from the fanciful and flinched as a branch slashed the windshield in front of her.

"The island has been pretty much deserted since the fish packing plant closed," he replied. "There was no need to keep the roads in repair...nor funding to do it. Just take it easy. You'll be fine. I've walked the trails. There aren't any major potholes or other hazards that can damage a vehicle."

An image of this handsome, virile creature roaming the deserted island in the fog and mist with his wolf dog by his side washed across her mind.

Get a grip on reality, Danielle.

"It's not much further, by my calculations." His voice snapped her back to the moment.

"Good. I don't fancy driving for miles through this labyrinth. It's amazing that an elderly lady like Hester Matthews could survive out here."

"She had excellent backup in Jimmy Waters. He took good care of her, from what Wade tells me."

The Mountie again. That's the last person I want to discuss. Or get involved with.

A few yards farther, the forest ended and the wheel tracks emerged into a field her headlights showed to be full of frost-killed marsh grass and tangled nettles. The fog Jimmy Waters had sought to avoid had rolled in over the clearing to give it a surreal appearance. A few hundred yards ahead in the thickening twilight, a small square cottage with a weird pyramid of a roof that looked like a stunted version of a witch's hat stood out in a dark silhouette against a backdrop of ghostly mist. A few yards to the right was a small shed that she assumed housed the generator Jimmy Waters had mentioned.

Danielle's breath caught in her throat. This truly was the far end of nowhere, weird and awful. She couldn't possibly live here. She'd turn the car where the trail widened into the dooryard and drive...where? Back to the empty ferry landing with no way of getting off the island? Her fingers white-knuckled on the wheel as she braked to a jolting halt.

"This is unbelievable."

"What is it? Something on the road?"

"No...no." She hated the stuttering sounds she was making. "It's just...I didn't expect the cottage to be...so..."

"Lonely? Rundown? Must be a lot like the farm. That's how Wade described my place. It's on a cliff down shore." He settled back in the seat. "He also said he could see the cottage from my front window. I'll start putting on the lights at night. You'll be able to see them and know you're not alone."

"Thanks." She forced a smile in his direction before remembering he couldn't see it. "Well." She heaved a sigh. "Better take a closer look."

She eased her foot off the brake and drove slowly toward the cottage. Thorns and nettles scraped against the car. In the sandy dooryard she stopped the vehicle and left the engine running as her headlights illuminated the place.

Alone on a bleak stretch of shoreline, the cottage at close range was even less appealing. Its cedar shingles, weathered to a ragged and variegated gray, made the place look as neglected as the houses in Cavalier's Cove. The white paint that had once been its trim had cracked and peeled until only a few tattered remains clung to window finishing, doorframe, and corner boards. Three rickety plank steps led up to a meter-square back stoop where a screen door clung crookedly on sagging hinges. A ragged dishcloth hung from a clothesline, supported by gnarled poles, that stretched across the sandy yard to the edge of the weed-infested field.

"We're here," she breathed. "For what it's worth."

"Dilapidated?"

"That's putting it optimistically." She couldn't believe Harry expected her to live in such a place. "It's…oh, my God!"

From a window near the door, two glowing yellow

eyes stared out into her car's headlights.

"What?" He shot bolt upright. "What?"

"Something is inside! It's staring out at us!"

Chapter Two

"That's impossible!" Andrew Drack faced straight ahead. "With the exception of a few mice, birds, and bats, there are only three living creatures on Phantom Island, and they're all in this car."

"Bats!"

"Calm down. There's only a few, and they're pretty reticent when it comes to people. Just don't leave any doors or windows without screens open...especially at night."

"Okay, so maybe there are only three considerable flesh-and-blood creatures." She fought to control the tremor in her voice. "But this place may have more than one phantom haunting it. I can't possibly stay."

"I thought you planned to photograph ghosts."

He turned toward her, and she saw what she read as suspicion slide over his face.

"Yes...yes, of course." *Get a grip. This man's friend is an RCMP constable. I can't afford to make him curious about me.* "I just didn't expect to encounter one so soon...or close at hand. I thought they stayed out on the water...or up the beach. I didn't think there would be one in my rental."

The eyes in the window disappeared. She didn't know whether to be relieved or more apprehensive. When they'd been peering out the window, she'd known the thing's exact location. Now whoever or

28

whatever possessed them could be anywhere.

"There isn't." He relaxed back into the seat. "There's a logical explanation."

" But those eyes… They glowed in my headlights."

"There's only one way to discover the truth. Lead me to the door."

"You mean we should go in?"

"Sure. I'll go first. It's a well established fact ghosts never harm blind people." In the shadowy darkness she saw a corner of his mouth quirk upward.

"You made that up!"

"Maybe. But doesn't the possibility that it might be true reassure you?" A grin settled in appealingly.

"Well…"

"Come on. Climb out of the car and lead me to the door. I promise you I'll do battle with any evil spirits as valiantly as a genuine exorcist." His grin moderated to take on a reassuring quality.

"Okay." She took a deep breath and turned off the engine. Leaving the headlights on so she could see her way, she opened her door, got out, and went around to where he was already standing beside the car.

"Let's go," he said, snapping open his cane.

"Should I let the dog out first?"

"That might be a good idea," he said. "Especially if you have food in there. I assume you brought groceries, and he hasn't had his dinner yet."

When Danielle opened the rear door, the dog burst past her like a great silver bullet.

"Fast, isn't he?" She struggled to regain her composure as the animal bounded around the cottage to disappear into the fog. "He won't run away, will he?"

"Don't worry. He's a working dog. He knows his

responsibilities. He'll stretch his legs and be right back. Now, let's get on with this ghost-busting business." He crooked an elbow in her direction.

She hesitated.

"Relax. It's easy. Take my arm. Lead the way. Don't worry. I'm getting good at not tripping over my own feet."

"I'm not experienced at this." She moved closer and put her fingers on his proffered arm.

"That makes two of us," he said, and she remembered Jimmy Waters' reference to Andrew Drack's blindness being the result of a recent accident. "We'll learn together, okay?"

"All right."

She let her fingers close over his arm. Together they crossed the sand and climbed the ragged steps. She released him to open the sagging screen door and insert the key into the weathered wooden one inside it. It swung inward with an eerie squeal.

"Oh!"

"Easy. It's nothing a drop of oil won't cure."

"Right." She drew a deep breath. "Be careful of the sill. It's warped."

Together they moved into the darkness. She was running a hand over the wall in search of a light switch when a venomous hissing stopped her.

"Snake!" She flattened herself against a wall.

Aladdin burst through the open doorway. An outraged yowl erupted. Furniture scraped and crashed. The room flooded with light.

Danielle saw Andrew a few feet away, his hand on a switch. Over in a corner Aladdin, barking furiously, had chased a small black cat to the top of a round-cornered refrigerator. The animal, bristled into a glowering, ebony ball, appeared ready to attack the dog with all the ferocity of a Tasmanian devil.

"Aladdin, come! Now!"

Muttering a growl, the dog moved to Andrew's side. The cat melted to normal size but remained hunched on its perch.

"Cat?" he asked.

"Yes, a small black one. It probably belonged to the cottage's former owner. Jimmy Waters said something about bringing Hester Matthew and a cat out here. When Miss Matthews took ill and had to be rushed off the island, it must have gotten left behind, outside where it was able to survive on rodents. It most likely sneaked inside yesterday while Jimmy was opening the place up."

"That explains the eyes in the window." Andrew Drack leaned against the wall and grinned. "I told you there'd be a logical explanation."

"Yes, well, this place doesn't have an ambience that encourages logical explanations."

"Relax. Tell me what it's like in here. Dirty, empty, what?"

"No." She looked around at the kitchen that stretched across the back of the cottage. "It's just musty and kind of weirdly old-fashioned."

"Describe."

"Well, there's a big cooking range, and a vintage round-cornered refrigerator that is currently topped with one little black cat, lots of chipped white cupboards, a wooden dining set with ladderback chairs painted fire-engine red, and a window over the sink that looks east, probably toward your house. The floor is worn gray plank. There's a doorway straight ahead that probably leads to the living room. Let me find another light switch and I'll know for sure."

"See? You're fine now," he commented as she headed further into the cottage. "Tell me about the rest of the place."

"Retro seventies, I'd say." Danielle found another switch and gazed around the front room. "Pine walls, couch and chairs sporting the biggest, wildest floral designs I've ever seen, an abused coffee table, an overflowing bookcase, and two big picture windows on either side of the front door that must look onto the beach. Presently they're covered with gold-colored drapes. Over in a far corner is an ancient rolltop desk holding what I believe is a CB radio. There's a fieldstone fireplace to the left that looks as if it still can be used."

"A fireplace? Aladdin, stay." Swinging his cane in front of him, he left the dog in the kitchen and came to join her. "Is there any wood? You need a fire. It's cold as a crypt in here."

"Thanks for that heartwarming analogy."

"Sorry. I go a lot on feelings now. What about that wood?"

"There's a big box with logs, kindling, and newspapers on the right of it. Do you know how to make a fire?"

"I was an Eagle Scout. Take me to the hearth and bring on the makings."

"This way." She took his arm and led him forward. "Careful, we've arrived. Fireplace at twelve o'clock."

He knelt and felt about until his hand encountered the woodbox. Watching him build the makings of a fire with such obvious expertise, Danielle was amazed.

"You're good at this."

"Told you I was an Eagle Scout. Match?" He held out a hand.

"I don't smoke."

"You're telling me you came to an isolated cottage without any matches?"

"Well, I figured generator, gas stove…"

"And exactly how did you intend to ignite that gas?"

"I…I don't know!" She swung away from him, exasperated with herself, with him, with everything. She didn't need this stranger treating her like an ill-prepared fool. "Why don't you just go back to your farmhouse and leave me to manage my incompetence alone?"

"Hey, hey, take it easy." He got to his feet and stood facing her. "I didn't mean to upset you."

"Don't be condescending!"

"I'm not. Believe me, I've had enough of that attitude these last few months myself."

"Sorry, sorry." She turned away.

"Don't be. We're just two people feeling lost and lonely on a dreary night in the middle of nowhere." His voice took on a soft, seductive tone. "Offering each other support and solace can't be wrong, can it?"

She hesitated. "Probably not."

"Okay, let's get you set up. There's bound to be matches in the kitchen, probably somewhere near the stove, in a jar to keep them dry and out of the clutches of mice."

"I'll take a look." As she started to leave the room, she paused.

"Would you like to stay to dinner? It won't be elegant, but it will save you the trouble of making a meal when I drive you back to your farmhouse."

"I'd be delighted, ma'am." Again that slow, arousing smile beneath the glasses. *God, I wish I could see his eyes. So much of a person's character can be read in their eyes…maybe even blind ones.*

It took only a few seconds for her to locate the jar containing the matches, found as he'd suggested on a shelf beside the stove. She opened it and returned to the living room.

"Your matches, sir."

"Thank you." He took the jar, extracted one, and knelt again by the hearth to scratch it on the stones. When it ignited, he leaned forward, located a piece of paper protruding from the pile of wood and kindling, and touched the flame to it. A blaze sprang up.

"Wonderful!" *At last, something warm and positive in this cold, bleak day.*

He threw another log into the flames and stood.

"The next order of business is to get my friend Constable Wade James on the CB and have him assure you of my reliability." He rubbed his hands together. "Take me to your radio. I have to check in with the constable anyway. I've promised him I'll call every evening to let him know I'm all right. He tends to be a worrier." He smiled.

"Okay, fine."

"Come on, lead me to that radio, and we'll get that bit of business out of the way."

****

"Andy? Are you okay? I was beginning to worry. You're calling. Over." The professionally strong, no-

34

nonsense voice of the RCMP constable emanated from the radio in the corner of the room.

"I'm fine, Wade." Seated on a frail-looking ladderback chair in front of the device, Andrew Drack flicked a switch and spoke. "Just wanted you to know I have company. A Ms. Dani Breckenreid has moved into the cottage. She's a photographer, here to take pictures of local ghosts. I'm at the Matthews place with her now. Over."

"Jimmy Waters told me he'd gotten a request to take a lady out to the island. So she's with you? Over."

"Yes, here at the cottage. Over."

"Thanks for filling me in. Now, if there's nothing else, I have to get back to work. Over."

"Before you go, will you speak to Ms. Breckenreid and tell her she's safe in my company? She needs peace of mind to get a good night's rest. Over."

"Surely. Miss Breckenreid, can you hear me? Over."

Danielle hesitated before bending over Andrew's shoulder toward the microphone.

"Yes, Constable. Over."

"Andy Drack is completely trustworthy," the strong, cool voice replied. "You're as safe under his protection as if you had your own private security guard. Sleep well. Over."

"Thanks, Constable, I'll try. Over."

"And out." Andrew Drack shut off the CB and leaned back in his chair. "Reassured?"

"I guess."

****

Later they sat before a crackling fire finishing the last of the ham sandwiches and coffee Danielle had made. Her suitcase was stowed away in the small cubicle that served as a bedroom, her toiletries in the bathroom with its narrow shower stall, and wall-hung washbasin, her groceries in refrigerator and cupboard.

"I'm sorry I didn't have anything more suitable for the dog," she said as she watched the animal gulping down a sandwich. "I gave the cat a can of tuna and some milk on top of the refrigerator. She still refuses to come down."

"A bowl of water and a sandwich are Aladdin's idea of a gourmet treat." Andrew Drack bent and began to untie his sneakers. "Is it okay if I take off my shoes? They're soaked, and the idea of warming my feet in front of a wood fire is mighty appealing."

"That sounds like an excellent idea." Danielle bent over her own laces. "I've had these running shoes on since seven a.m. May I ask a personal question?"

"Sure." He placed his footwear in front of the fire and settled back. "Whether I choose to answer is another matter."

"I don't understand why a…blind person would choose to come here to live. You're so alone with only yourself and the dog to depend on."

"That's exactly the reason." He stretched his feet out toward the fire. "I have to prove to myself I can be independent. What better place than this?"

"How did you know about Phantom Island? It isn't exactly highlighted on tourist maps."

"Wade James. He and I have been friends since University. When I visited him here last spring I was impressed by the picturesque isolation of the place and of this island in particular. After the accident, when I needed a proving ground, this spot sprang to mind. I'd be alone and yet Wade would be only a CB call away if anything went really wrong."

"I'm surprised your friend would agree."

"At first he didn't. But then he found me a companion...Aladdin. The dog was Wade's birthday gift to me a month after the accident." He stretched forward to rub the animal's head.

"Where did he find a qualified dog so quickly? I thought there were long waiting lists for seeing-eye dogs."

"Aladdin was unique." Andrew Drack leaned back on the couch and continued his story. "He'd been trained as a guide dog but had proven a bit too aggressive for the work. Because of this tendency, he was handed over to the RCMP. After re-training, he proved insufficiently assertive for their program. Caught between two jobs, his future, at that point, looked pretty bleak."

"Why?" Danielle picked up the coffeepot from where she'd left it warming on the hearth and replenished their cups.

"Once attack trained, a dog isn't considered a candidate for regular adoption. Wade heard about the dog's predicament, decided he was just what I needed, and bought him for me."

"Worked out beautifully for both of you."

"It surely did." He stretched, about to get up. "But I'm telling stories, and you must be tired. Did you have a long drive today?"

"Yes." Instantly Danielle was alert. "From Ottawa." The lie flew out.

"That *is* a long haul. What is it, ten or twelve hours?"

"Roughly." Danielle stretched and yawned. *Not so hard, lying, once you get the hang of it.*

"Bed is definitely next on your agenda," he said matter-of-factly and reached for his sneakers. "So I'll say good night and head for home."

"I'll drive you." She started to get up.

"That isn't necessary." He shoved his feet into his sneakers. "I'd be uneasy about your returning here alone. You're not familiar with the lanes. In the mist and dark you could get confused."

"And go where? A half mile or so in the wrong direction? Phantom Island isn't exactly the size of New Zealand."

"No, but it can be a pretty spooky place at night." He tied his laces, his fingers deftly completing the task.

"That fact doesn't seem to bother you."

"Hey, like I've told you, ghosts almost never bother blind people." He shot one of his heart-melting grins in her direction as he stood. "Now if you'll just hand me my jacket…"

She retrieved it from the back of a chair.

"Thanks." He shrugged into it. "Aladdin, come. It's time to take us home."

The dog moved obediently to his side. He pulled the lead from his pocket and, finding the dog's collar, snapped it in place.

"Now if you'll head us outside, we'll make our way up the beach." He took out his cane and opened it.

"If you're certain you'll be okay…" She opened the door and stepped aside so that he and the dog could exit.

"Quite certain. Sleep well…Dani Breckenreid."

Spoken with a soft sensuousness, the words sent a

shiver coursing over her.

"And you as well." She forced out a response.

She followed him out onto the veranda to watch him and the dog go down the steps and start up the beach.

The fog was lifting, lying in gossamer strips low above beach and ocean. Andrew Drack and his wolf creature appeared ghosts themselves as they walked through it. The moon appeared, turning retreating clouds into grayish white ghosts drifting silently across the pitch-black sky.

As she watched man and dog make their way down the beach, a movement on the cliff down the shore caught her attention. She gasped. On the promontory near a dark silhouette she guessed was Andrew's farmhouse, she saw them...a horse and rider. The animal reared against the face of the moon, his rider's cape billowing, a plume on his wide-brimmed hat fluttering. A swath of clouds swung across the moon, concealing the pair. When it passed, they'd vanished.

For a moment she could only stare at the point where they'd suddenly appeared and just as suddenly vanished. Finally, coming out of shock, she raced down the veranda steps and up the beach after the man and dog.

"Andrew!" she yelled.

He turned and waited.

Reaching him, she grasped his arm so tightly he winced.

"Dani, what in God's name..."

"Andrew, I saw him...it...the ghost...and his horse...just now on the cliff near your house! His horse reared against the full moon, and then clouds passed over the moon and he…they were gone!"

"Calm down. It's just this place. It can play tricks on people…at least, that's what those who can see tell me. It's only the fog. It moves and churns and seems to take on shapes, I've been told."

"No, no, no!" She shook his arm. "This wasn't any wreathing bit of mist. It was a clear image…a man in a cape and wearing a wide-brimmed hat! And a horse, a big dark horse!"

"Let me walk you back to your cottage. I think I'd better spend the night on your couch. Tomorrow, in daylight, you'll realize all your night fears were fakes working on a brain that's overtired after a long day."

"No!" She released him and lurched away. "Just because you can't see what I've witnessed doesn't mean it doesn't exist! Go back to your farmhouse! I hope the phantom rattles your windows and moans around it all night!"

"Dani, be sensible. It was only a figment of your imagination."

Ignoring the plea in his voice, she whirled and ran, stumbling over driftwood, tangling her ankles in seaweed, back to her cottage and up the steps. Inside, she slammed the door and bolted it.

He doesn't believe me. I'm alone, at the mercy of whoever or whatever that thing on the cliff is.

She sank down on the worn couch, clutching a pillow to her chest.

I have to get away from this insane island. I can't stay here a minute longer.

She jumped to her feet and headed for the bedroom. She was snapping the lock on her suitcase when a semblance of reason returned.

Oh, God, oh, God! This isn't the answer. She stopped, threw back her head, closed her eyes, and sucked in a gulp of air. *I have to think, think, think.*

Fighting to bring her somersaulting thoughts under control, she launched into the deep breathing exercises her yoga instructor had taught her as a method of relaxing and finding stability.

The application worked. As common sense returned, she knew that flight was out of the question. *If I leave this island, a jail cell will be a very real possibility. I have to stay calm and wait to hear from Harry. Yes, that's it. Stay calm and wait for Harry.*

Regaining self-control, she drew in deep breaths and slowly released them. Closing her eyes, she tried to conjure up images of handsome, charismatic Doctor Harry Stone...images of them on a romantic expedition to Egypt, of them sharing adventures under a desert sun, far away from the ghostly fogs and phantoms of this miserable little island. It proved difficult. Harry's image wouldn't come into clear focus.

With a sigh, she curled up on the couch and gazed at her moldering surroundings. How long would she be forced to stay in this forlorn little dustbin? Harry had said he'd get her out of this mess. But would he? How well did she really know Harry Stone? He'd come into her life such a short time ago. His professional reputation was impeccable, but what about his character? What kind of man was he, really?

I'm losing it, going mad under the strain. Of course Harry will get me exonerated of the charges. And of course he'll come for me. But right now, I'm tired, so tired...

She stood and walked into the shabby bedroom

with its dusty furniture. The bed, although made up neatly, emitted a musty odor. Maybe with clean bedding it would be okay. She'd seen a washing machine in a corner of the kitchen. Hopefully it worked.

The small bathroom proved to be an equally stale room. The shower stall, rimmed with graying soap buildup, had a cobweb hanging diagonally across one corner of its door. Turning on the grungy washbasin's tap, she released a gush of repressed air that made her jump back before water burst out in fits and starts.

Well, it looks clean. And the towels don't appear dirty. Nevertheless, they'll get a laundering in the morning. Right now I need sleep.

She bent over the sink and splashed water over her face, then used a small, cracked bar of soap beside it to wash more thoroughly. Holding her breath, she rubbed herself dry. She couldn't bear any odors of abandonment and disuse she guessed the towel might give off. Opening her makeup case, she took out her toothpaste and brush and cleaned her teeth. .

She paused in the bedroom and looked at her suitcase where she'd left it against the wall. *I won't unpack. I won't be here long enough to settle in. Harry will clear my name, and I'll be able to go home again.* Grabbing an afghan that had been draped over the end of the bed, she gave it a shake, sneezed as dust scattered, then headed back to the living room.

Leaving a lamp burning, she added another log to the dying fire, replaced the screen in front of it, and curled up on the couch. She'd barely closed her eyes when a small thump near her feet made her bolt upright. A soft meow greeted her. The little black cat stared up at her, wide-eyed.

"Were you lonely all by yourself up there on the refrigerator?" she asked, stretching a cautious hand to pet its head. "Do you want to be friends?"

A soft purr accompanied her caress.

"Okay, let's settle down to have a good night's rest. You can be guard cat."

Although she meant the last facetiously, she had to admit she did feel better with the small, warm body curled up behind her knees.

Chapter Three

Danielle awoke to a shaft of sunlight streaming in through a small opening between the living room drapes and then sniffed the odor of stale house. She stared up at the pyramid ceiling as the reality of her situation slid back over her. Why couldn't she wake up from the terrible nightmare her life had become? She sucked in a deep breath and tried to resign herself to her fate: *Well, since that isn't going to happen, I may as well get on with the day.*

Sitting up, she shoved aside the afghan that had been her bedding and snapped off the lamp. At the end of the couch, the cat yowled, stood, and arched its back.

"Sorry to disturb you," she addressed it. "I guess you did a good job as watch cat. I survived the night." Yawning and stretching, she headed for the bathroom.

This place needs some serious cleaning. She slapped aside the spider web that curtained the shower stall and began to shed her rumpled clothes. *Maybe tidied and dusted this old place won't be so bad for a few days...a very few days. If I don't hear from Harry by the weekend, I'm leaving. I can't stay indefinitely on this haunted scrap of land with a satanically handsome blind man, his wolf dog, and a phantom horseman as companions.* Resolved, she stepped into the stall and was relieved when hot water gushed out of the rusted showerhead.

Wrapped in a towel, she returned to the bedroom, threw her suitcase onto the bed, and snapped it open. Looking over the contents, she heaved a sigh. Sexy underwear and nightgowns, dresses, pants, skirts, and tops—all were chosen for a romantic city weekend and weren't suited for this place. She rummaged through the soft, sensual garments and found a pair of jeans, a sweatshirt, and cotton socks she'd ferreted away just in case she and Harry decided to take a hike along any of the trails the Montreal area was famous for.

She shook them out and dressed. Feeling marginally better, she went back into the living room, pulled open the drapes, and blinked.

Really? Here again?

Andrew Drack and his wolf dog sat on her veranda steps. In the October sunlight the handsome man in a tan barn coat and jeans, with dog beside him, both facing out toward the sun-dappled bay, appeared like an ad in an outdoor clothing magazine. Had she imagined the pair's unnerving ambience the previous night? Had nerves and fatigue made them seem more darkly fascinating and mysterious than they actually were? Or—she stumbled over the thought—were they like Dr. Jekyll and Mr. Hyde, exuding one persona at night and another by day?

Don't be absurd. You're letting your imagination run wild...again.

Forcing thoughts of the previous night to the back of her mind, she stepped out onto the veranda. It ran across the entire front of the cottage and offered a panoramic view of the Atlantic stretching to the horizon.

"Good morning. Did you sleep well?"

"Decently." He turned and smiled up in the direction of her voice. The dog muttered something in its throat. "You?"

"The same. What time is it?"

"Seven or thereabouts," he said.

"You're an early riser." She took a deep breath of crisp, salt-tinged air.

"An old habit. Used to enjoy watching the sun rise."

"It's a gorgeous one." She moved to lean over the veranda railing and survey the beach stretched out before her. With its seaweed-and-driftwood-punctuated expanse, the golden-sanded beach would have sent artists or photographers with a bent for pristine seascapes scuttling to capture its natural beauty. "Sunny and warm, with just a hint of a breeze ruffling the water."

"Hey, I know that! I can still feel the sun on my face and the wind in my hair."

"I thought you said you slept well."

"I did."

"Then why are you so cranky?"

He lowered his head and shook it slowly.

"You're right. I am cranky. I'm still having trouble adjusting to my present condition. Bear with me?"

He looked up at her, and her heart did something crazy like skip a beat. She hesitated.

"Well?"

"Sure, why not? How about toast and coffee?" She had to struggle to sound flip and casual.

"Sounds good. Should we wait out here? I'm not sure if Aladdin and your cat have come to terms for island cohabitation."

"My cat?" She stopped with her hand on the screen door handle. "It's...it was Hester Matthews' cat."

"Wrong. She's gone and you fed it. That means you've adopted it. All that's left to do is to name it."

"Don't hold your breath."

Letting the door bang shut behind her, she turned back into the living room.

Inside, the cat sat perched on the coffee table. She looked up at Danielle with round, curious eyes.

"Should we trust them?" she asked softly, beneath Andrew's hearing.

The little cat muttered and turned away.

"You're right. We'll take it slow and easy."

****

She returned to the porch carrying a tray with two mugs of coffee and a plate stacked with buttered toast.

"Smells good," he commented as she sat down beside him and placed the meal between them.

She hesitated, took his hand, and touched his fingers to the handle of one of the mugs. "It's black, like last night."

"Perfect."

"Have some toast. Maybe you're hungry and that's what's putting your nose out of joint." She nudged the plate against him and, when he reached for it, again guided his hand. A tingle started from the point of contact.

How can guiding a man's hand to food and drink feel like an erotic touch?

"Could be. I've never handled hunger well." He took a slice, leaned back, and bit into it. Aladdin nudged him with a nose against his arm, and he laughed, a deep genuine sound like the husky, sensuous

47

chuckle of the previous night that had set her senses vibrating.

"Okay, okay. Ask Dani if I can share with you."

"Of course."

"Aladdin thanks you." He gave the dog a quarter slice.

They shared the rest of their breakfast in silence. Danielle was content to enjoy the view. Beyond the bright beach sand, a sapphire sky stooped to meet the charcoal-blue bay trimmed with frothy little whitecaps that danced and glistened in the sunshine. A light breeze, full of that unique essence that comes only from the sea, was cool enough to be invigorating without causing a chill. It scuttled among the patchy clumps of frost-browned marsh grass between cottage and shore, tugging at the tough old vegetation. The beauty of the scene made her adventure of the previous night seem a mere figment of an overtired, stressed mind.

She looked down shore and saw what she assumed was the farmhouse about a quarter mile away. Half hidden in a grove of wind-disfigured spruce on that infamous cliff, gray and weathered, with a mansard roof, it appeared fit only for the set of a horror movie or a residence for one of the island's paranormal inhabitants.

"What's keeping you so quiet? What are you looking at?" His words brought her back to the moment.

"Your home…" She fumbled. "Isn't far away."

"You can see it from here?"

"Most of it," she replied. "The back is hidden in the trees."

"Interesting." He stood. "Aladdin and I had better

be going. You have a lot of settling in to do. You'll also probably want to start scouting for photo locations. May I suggest a place where you'll have a good shot at the ghost…if he appears again?"

The hint of humor in his last sentence rankled her.

"I'm perfectly capable of finding a good location, thank you."

"Okay, okay, truce. I'm picturing you bristling like your cat."

"I can see you're in an annoyingly jocular mood now that you've had food…and I'm not. I'll drive you home before I start giving this place a serious cleaning. And it's not *my* cat."

"That's not necessary." He stood and pulled a leash from the pocket of his coat. "Aladdin can guide me well enough on the beach. I need the exercise. I've taken to spending too much time sitting around the house. Here's how to reach me by CB." He pulled a piece of paper with a few scrawled words on it from his jacket pocket. "I hope you can read it. I haven't done much writing lately. Call if you need me."

"I will."

"Thanks for breakfast. Come on, Aladdin. Home, boy."

She watched him limp down to the beach, the dog's leash in one hand, his white cane in the other. A lonely figure against the vastness of sea and sand, Andrew Drack personified the description of a man of mystery.

Enough speculating about my neighbor. I have cleaning to do. It will fill the time while I'm waiting for Harry to get in touch.

The cat got up from the coffee table, stretched, and

leaped to the floor as Danielle reentered the living room. She looked up, meowed appealingly, and Danielle saw it for the first time.

"You've got a white bib!" She leaned down and petted the ivory-colored splotch beneath the little animal's chin. "You're not really a black cat after all. I'll take that as a good omen and call you Bibsy."

The cat opened its mouth and yowled.

"Does that mean it's okay with you? Or are you simply hungry? I have lots of tuna. You'll have to survive on it until I put in an order with Jimmy Waters. That is, if you plan to live with me."

In answer, Bibsy yawned, stretched again, then, tail held high, strode regally toward the kitchen.

"May I take that as a yes?" Danielle shoved her hands into her jeans pockets and followed.

****

By noon the cottage's full inventory of towels and bedding were on the clothesline, fluttering in the breeze, the plank floors had been swept and mopped, the furniture dusted, and the kitchen and bathroom scrubbed.

Seated at the kitchen table, Danielle absently stirred her bowl of chunky vegetable soup and wondered if anything so full of unknown substances like those listed on the can could possibly have any food value.

Thinking of the unknown brought Harry Stone to mind. She bit into a cracker and leaned back in her chair. The museum's board of directors had considered obtaining the Egyptian display a major triumph and updated their security system in anticipation. The news that world-famous archeologist and adventurer Dr.

Harry Stone would escort the collection had been such an almost unbelievable bonus. The board had splurged on a champagne supper to celebrate their coup.

She'd been surprised when he'd asked her out to dinner the first night after his arrival. What could such a man of the world see in an archivist at a small East Coast museum?

Dr. Harrison, who'd known the archeologist for years, had assured her his interest was genuine, that Harry Stone was a fine man with a gentleman's reputation. But now she was in the worst trouble of her life, probably a whole lot more than what Dr. Harry Stone wanted to be involved in.

She looked down at the soup congealing in her bowl and grimaced. There was nothing she could do to remedy her situation until she heard from him. To fill the time, she decided, she'd read some of the old photography books she'd seen in the living room bookcase. Anything to keep her mind occupied. Engrossed in the idea, she started toward the sink to rinse her bowl.

Her foot hit something that yowled and leaped. Staggering back from the cat that had been sleeping at her feet, she toppled toward the table, its edge saving her from a fall. The half-empty bowl flew from her hands and landed on the faded area rug in front of the sink.

"Oh, no!" she wailed. "Look what you made me do!"

Bibsy leaped from floor to chair to cupboard to her safe haven atop the refrigerator. Round eyes casting a cold feline stare down on Danielle, she sat and began to pick bits of vegetables and noodles from her fur.

"Okay, okay, so I've got things to learn about living with a cat. You'll have to make allowances."

Danielle picked up the bowl and surveyed the spattered rug. "The best idea is to take it outside and scrub it. It appears due for a good cleaning anyway."

She placed the bowl in the sink, bent, and gave the bit of carpet a jerk. At first it stuck but finally flew up, producing a cloud of dust that made her cough and sneeze. As the dirt settled she saw a tarnished ring set flush into the floor beneath. Around it, in a four-foot square, were cuts through the floorboards.

A secret compartment! She stepped back to survey the hatch. *No telling what might be under it. Something shocking. Or horrendous. Like a dead body. Or a whole stack of dead bodies! Maybe Hester Matthews was some sort of kinky serial killer!*

As rationality returned, she put her hands on her hips and shook her head.

Get over yourself. You're letting this place do a number on you.

She grasped the loop and pulled.

Heavier than it looks.

She yanked harder, and the hatch yielded on silent hinges. Danielle held her breath as she eased it wide open.

Nothing sprang out. Nothing, that is, except a strange chemical odor mixed with a damp mustiness. A flight of crude wooden steps led downward into a cavern hollowed out of the earth. In the sunlight flooding the kitchen, she saw a light bulb suspended from the ceiling of the underground room, near the top of the narrow stairs. Bending forward on her knees, she pulled its chain. A weak-watted bulb winked on.

In its dim glow, she saw an earthen-floored and walled cubicle no more than eight feet square, barely high enough for a six-foot person to stand. A counter with a sink and a series of rusting metal trays ran along one side; a sort of clothesline hung across its center.

"A darkroom! Of course!" she explained to the cat who had come to peer down into the space beside her. "Hester Matthews must have developed photos down there when she used film-type cameras."

She shivered. The elderly photographer might have been comfortable in that dank, windowless hole, but she never would be. The mere thought of descending into the clammy, dungeon-like space was enough to make her sweat and start her heart banging at her ribs. Easing the hatch closed, she decided to put that ugly black hole out of her mind.

****

An hour later she glanced out the kitchen window. The topmost gable window of the farmhouse showed above the trees. In an effort to forget about the small dungeon under her kitchen, she turned her thoughts to her handsome, mysterious neighbor. Did Andrew like home cooking? Should she invite him for a meal before she left the island?

On second thought, she decided against the idea. He'd come here seeking solitude to come to grips with his handicap. His solicitousness in helping her settle into the cottage in no way meant he wanted to start a friendship.

Anyhow, staying away from him was probably a good idea. His best friend was the local RCMP constable. She might let something incriminating slip in the course of conversation. She crossed her fingers and hoped that Wade James wouldn't take it into his head to check on her story about being an Ottawa photographer.

I have to get practical and start working on my photographer ruse. The logical place to start is with that bunch of photography books stuffed into the shelves of the living room bookcase. Even though they're old and outdated, they might provide some idea of concepts like depth of field and composition and other aspects I've heard photographers visiting the museum talk about. Maybe after some intense reading I'll be able to pass myself off as a photographer if Wade James or Andrew Drack decide to question me on the subject.

****

At five thirty she put aside a book on night photography, got up from the couch, and stretched. Her reading had been enlightening. Although most of the publications were geared for film cameras, stuck in among the pages of several she'd found old newspaper articles describing sightings of the Fire Ship. According to the stories, the Ship with its sails blazing, phantom sailors desperately climbing the rigging to escape the flames, had appeared at various times, at all seasons, even seemingly gliding over the ice in the dead of winter, but it had most frequently been seen in late October.

Bibsy, who had been curled up beside her, looked up expectantly and opened her mouth in a loud, plaintive meow.

"Food time again?" She realized how glad she was to have the cat as a companion. At least it kept her from talking to the walls. Maybe Andrew Drack talked to Aladdin...aside from giving him commands.

Thinking of him sent a quiver of excitement dancing through her body. He was the most intriguing man she'd met in many moons...except Harry, of course. But Harry lacked Andrew Drack's dark charisma, that mysterious something that was as nebulous as it was sensual and which his blindness in no way diminished.

In fact, his lack of sight gave him added appeal. It made him different, not just another handsome hunk. And, she thought, feeling cruelly selfish, it kept him from discovering just how plain and unglamorous Dani Breckenreid really was. That weekend in Montreal with Harry had been meant to be her first foray into being overtly romantic and sexy.

Enough fantasizing. Time to get back to the moment and some serious planning.

She placed a bowl of tuna in front of Bibsy. The prospect of another night alone in the cottage with the cat as her only companion wasn't as terrifying as she'd thought it would be. The fine, bright autumn day had done much to expunge her first impression of the island's sinister atmosphere. The place had a wild, unspoiled beauty under clear skies and sunshine. Even the memory of the ghostly horseman had faded in its ability to horrify her. Probably, as Andrew had said, it was just a trick of fog, moonlight, and shadow.

"In fact," she said to Bibsy, "I think I'll try some night photography. That book I read today laid out the basics of composition and time exposure. Since I am supposedly here to get a photo of the Fire Ship, I'll need evidence of having at least made an attempt."

****

She waited until ten thirty before pulling on her

faux suede jacket and gathering up the camera and tripod. *Here goes nothing.* Squaring her shoulders, she opened the cottage door on a night as still as death. As she paused at the top of the steps, frosty air brushed her face. Looking out over the ocean, she saw the moon reflected in the black, still water. Seaweed and driftwood cast twisted shadows over the pale sand.

Perfect setting for any ghost.

She hesitated, waffling in the eerie ambience. Glancing to her right, she saw Andrew's house in dark silhouette. If he could live on Phantom Island alone and handicapped, she should be able to manage. Resolve renewed, she set off across the beach, the only sound that of her sneakers crunching the cold sand.

Reaching a spot she thought would suit her purposes, she planted the tripod in the sand and screwed the camera in place. Satisfied with the setup, she put her eye to the viewfinder and began panning over beach and bay. At first she saw only the dark water, the silver-charcoal sky, and long stretches of shadowed beach.

A slight noise made her turn, and her breath caught in her throat. Thirty feet behind her, mounted on his horse amid the ragged marsh grass, was the Phantom. The horse steamed in the cold air, forming a vaporous nimbus. Sound muted in her throat; mobility deserted her body.

The Phantom swept off his plumed hat and saluted her with a deep bow. A bandana and mask covered his hair and the top half of his face. Before she could come out of the trance his appearance had cast over her, he swung the horse about and galloped away through the grass and into the ragged blackness of the trees.

Danielle clapped a hand to her throat. She had seen

the Phantom at close range. He was real. With an agonized cry, she abandoned her camera equipment and, tripping over driftwood and dead grasses, ran stumbling back to the cottage.

As she floundered up the veranda steps, she tripped and fell full length on its planks. With a yowl, she scrambled to her feet and lunged for the door. Inside, she whirled to shove the deadbolt into place. Her body heaving, she threw her back against the panel and slid down its length.

Oh, God, oh, God! She trembled violently, her teeth chattering, as she crouched on the floor, arms clasped around her drawn-up knees. *There really is a Phantom, and he really does ride the beaches at night. I didn't imagine him. This time I met him up close and personal...*

Bibsy, curled up in a corner of the couch, stared at her with round, yellow eyes. For a single paranoid moment Danielle fancied the cat a partner to the apparition she'd seen, a bit of its macabre spirit lurking within her own home.

Get a grip. All you saw was some kind of crazy light-and-shadow show. There are no such things as ghosts. Definitely not one from a shipwreck three hundred years ago. She released her clasped hands and moved them to massage the tightness at the back of her neck. *Think, think. Andrew. Call Andrew on the CB and tell him. Tell him what? That I've seen a ghost...again? A specter he'd think was another figment of an overly zealous ghost hunter's imagination? No, I can't call Andrew Drack.*

She pulled herself to her feet and went to check the back door lock on legs that had barely more strength than Jell-O. By the time she'd finished with the windows and had made certain the drapes were closed, her strength was returning.

I'm going to be fine, just fine. But a little Dutch courage won't hurt. She went to the refrigerator and took out one of the bottles of wine she'd purchased with her groceries on her way to the island and, rummaging in first one and then another untidy kitchen drawer, found a corkscrew.

What a wimp! If my hands don't stop shaking, I'll be drinking bits of cork.

A quick search of disorganized cupboards revealed only more mess and no wine glasses. *Damn it! Is there nothing right about this place? I bet if Bibsy hadn't been in residence, I'd be finding mice. Yuck!*

She selected a water tumbler, rinsed it at the sink, and carried it and the bottle into the living room. With a muttered expletive, she sank down on the couch.

"Here's to us, Bibsy." She saluted the cat with the bottle. "Genuine survivors, right?"

The cat watched with feline intensity as Danielle poured the glass half full, took a long, slow drink, then settled back with sigh. For a few moments they sat in silence.

"It was only shadows." When she spoke to the cat again, her words bumped a little. She'd never drunk so much wine so fast, but she was beginning to feel better. "The Headless Horseman still in possession of his head isn't likely to be here on Phantom Island, is he? Naw! There aren't enough people to provide a decent audience for a respectable spook. Jimmy Waters said he hasn't been seen in over fifty years. He's not likely to show up now, just for my benefit, is he?" She took another long sip, laughed, hiccupped, and reached for the bottle.

****

Like a shadow, the horseman emerged from the grove of black spruce behind her cottage. He halted his horse and leaned forward over the pommel of his saddle to watch and wait. The curtains were drawn on all the windows, but cracks of light around them suggested she was still awake. Beneath him, the stallion shifted restlessly. Shaking its head, the animal rattled its bit and blew steam into the cold air.

"Quiet, Cavalier."

He dismounted and tied his mount to a tree. As quiet and ethereal as a shadow, he headed for the old car parked near the back door. It took him only a few tries to release the lock on the trunk. He pulled out a small light and looked inside. It had been cleaned for sale as best such an old vehicle could be. A spare tire, a jack, and a tire wrench lay to one side.

He ran his gloved hand around the edge of the worn carpet until his fingers encountered a slight rise. Carefully he lifted upward. His breath caught at what he found hidden beneath. He stared down at the contents and saw the future.

Tonight won't be the last time you'll see me, Dani Breckenreid or whatever your name is. Oh, no, definitely not.

He adjusted his plumed hat, drew his cloak more closely about him, and glanced at the cottage. A light flicked out in the kitchen. She was probably going to bed. As quietly as he'd come, he remounted, turned his horse toward the trees, and melted back into the shadows.

Chapter Four

" Dani, are you in there?"

Andrew Drack's voice hurt but roused her out of a deep sleep. As a nauseating pain burst from somewhere behind her eyes, she opened them and grimaced. When she tried to reply, her mouth parchment dry, she could only croak.

She hadn't felt this bad since one morning at university after a friend had talked her into sharing a two-liter bottle of cheap red wine. In the dimness of a room with its drapes still drawn against the morning light, she saw the empty bottle on the coffee table.

Oh, God, I must have drunk the entire thing and passed out on the couch.

"Dani! Are you in there? Are you okay?" There was a knock on the door.

With a moan, she struggled upright on the couch, dislodging Bibsy, who had been curled up behind her knees. The little cat yowled and leaped to the floor.

"Dani!" He banged more loudly.

"Coming." *Stop that infernal hammering!* She stumbled to her feet. Her head pounded as she made her way to the front door. When she opened it, the blast of early morning sunlight that hit her full in the eyes sent a wave of nausea crashing over her.

"Excuse me." She whirled and made a beeline for the bathroom.

****

By the time she was ready to return to the living room, her face tingling from the gallons of cold water she'd splashed over it, her system beginning to absorb the aspirin and anti-nausea pill she'd swallowed, she courted the idea that she might survive. She glanced into the mirror above the basin on her way to the door and shuddered.

Could I possibly look worse? And I've slept in my clothes...

For a single, selfish second she was glad Andrew couldn't see.

Horrible, narcissistic creature. What a monstrous thought!

But he didn't have to know what had happened the previous night. She'd tell him she had a touch of food poisoning.

The lie died before she could bring it to life. As she stepped out into the living room, she saw him seated on the couch, dangling the empty wine bottle from his fingers between his spread knees as he sat hunched forward on the couch. Again wearing his barn coat and jeans, the man she was coming to think of as Daylight Andrew looked up at the sound of her entrance.

Aladdin, appearing as grim as his master, sat by his side. Bibsy had disappeared.

That's loyalty for you, leaving me when I need support.

"I smelled wine." He tapped the bottle with his fingers. "Do you have a problem with alcohol? Is that the reason you decided to isolate yourself out here? If so, bringing a stash with you won't help."

"No!" The word snapped out. Moderating her tone

61

she continued, "I just happen to enjoy red wine." *Why did he have to look so sexy in those jeans? Why couldn't he have been fat and ugly, a frog, not a prince. And why am I feeling embarrassed? What I do is none of his business.*

"Really? Well, then, let's crack another bottle and get right to it." He started to get up.

"No!" The mere thought of more wine headed her stomach toward another revolt.

"Look, there's no shame in admitting you were uneasy." His tone moderated as he settled back onto the couch. "I was, on my first night alone out here. The trick is not to allow irrational fears to get the better of you, or"—he set the wine bottle aside on the coffee table—"resorting to this." He got up and snapped open his cane. "Actually, to be rational about the situation, we're safer out here than anywhere on the mainland. There's only the four of us, and we're all one hundred percent trustworthy. At least, I know Aladdin and I are. That just leaves you and the cat."

His face relaxed into that grin Danielle found far too appealing.

"You're right." She drew a deep breath. "I *am* here to photograph a ghost. I can't afford to get skittish."

"You'll get over it. I did. Do you realize how cold it is in here?" He changed the subject. "Why don't I build a fire while you make toast and coffee? There's nothing like food and a little warmth to chase away the shakes."

"You're inviting yourself to breakfast?" She planted her hands on her hips and confronted him. "Seconds after you accuse me of being a lush? I like your style, mister."

"Hey, I'm the self-proclaimed Lord Mayor, Chief Justice, and CEO of this scrap of land. I do as I please." The grin below the dark glasses widened.

"I'm surprised you didn't simply declare yourself Emperor." *Good. Lightening the mood and moving on.*

"That would be undemocratic, especially now that I have a citizen. At the next election, please feel free to vote for the candidate of your choice."

Whistling, he headed for the woodbox in the corner, white cane tapping a path. Danielle stifled the desire to help, turned, and went into the kitchen. He was becoming familiar with the cottage. Best leave him alone.

"Matches are in the bottle on the mantel," she called back over her shoulder.

****

They were seated at the kitchen table with plates of scrambled eggs and toast when Aladdin, lying by Andrew's side, uttered a low growl.

"Cat?" Andrew paused as he started to pick up his coffee cup.

"Bibsy is on top of the refrigerator again. Apparently *she* doesn't consider one of us trustworthy."

"Bibsy?" Andrew's eyebrows went up above the rim of his glasses. "Where did that come from?"

"Her chest is white," Danielle replied, slathering strawberry jam on her toast. "As if she's wearing a little bib. Therefore, Bibsy."

"Cute." He took a drink.

"Don't be patronizing. You've got a dog named Aladdin. Suppose you explain that one."

"Because, like a lamp, he lights my way." The teasing went out of his tone as he put down his cup and turned his attention to his eggs.

"Andrew, I'm…"

She caught herself.

"No, I'm sorry." He toyed with the food on his plate. "We were enjoying a nice breakfast until I spoiled it with something that sounded like self-pity. Let's forget it and move on, okay?"

"Okay." She was relieved. They *really* did much better when she forgot he was blind.

"What scared you last night? Did the Fire Ship put in one of its rare appearances?" He returned his attention to his breakfast and spoke off-handedly.

"No. Andrew, promise you won't laugh or scoff or be condescending if I tell you the truth." In spite of her resolve not to tell him about her experience, she had to confide in someone, to talk about her sighting with another human being.

"Scout's honor." He made a sign she assumed sealed the bargain.

"Last night when I was on the beach with my camera, hoping to get a picture of the Fire Ship, I heard a rustle in the dried marsh grass behind me. When I turned to see what had caused it, he and his horse were only a few feet away." The words tumbled out in a rush.

"He?"

"The Phantom!" The words were a cry of exasperation. "Who do you think?"

"Did you get a picture?"

"What, no snide remark, no dispelling comments?"

"I was simply wondering if you'd gotten proof to show Wade. Maybe he'd be willing to investigate."

"Then you do believe me."

"I believe you saw something. Just what that something is remains to be determined. Now about that picture?"

"Oh, God!" Memory flooded back. "I left my camera and tripod on the beach. I was so panicked all I could think about was getting back to the cottage."

"Well, let's go and get it." He stood and snapped open his cane. "Maybe, in your surprise, you pressed the shutter. Maybe you have a picture of this mysterious night rider."

"Okay." She stood. "What do you know about the ghost and his horse?"

"This whole coast line is lousy with stories of ghosts and phantoms of one kind or another." He shrugged. "Probably what you saw was only a play of light and shadow…like you encountered the previous night."

"You're saying I imagined a horseman…twice?" She gathered up her dishes and headed for the sink. "I was only a few feet from him last night. I heard his horse blowing, saw both of them immersed in some sort of glowing cloud. Are you grinning? You promised you wouldn't scoff, Mr. Eagle Scout."

"I'm not scoffing, believe me. Probably what you saw was steam rising from the marshy ground. I'm told it can create strange illusions. Sorry if I appeared skeptical."

She swung back to face him and recognized sincerity in his expression.

"Now who's saying that word too often?"

"Okay, okay. As Lord Mayor, Chief Justice, and CEO of Phantom Island, I move we strike the word from our vocabulary once and for all."

"Aye and amen. On a positive note, you must be a bit curious to learn what my camera might have captured."

"If there was an actual ghost, legend declares, all you'll find is a black blank. Cameras are incapable of recording the paranormal."

"Actual ghost? For someone who doesn't believe in them, you're a fount of knowledge on the subject."

"I'm just saying…"

"And previously you *just* said there were only three of us on the island, then you moved to amend that figure to four when we discovered Bibsy. You seem adept at changing the census of Phantom Island whenever it suits your purposes."

"Ah, Dani, let's stop this pointless bickering and go get your camera." He heaved an exasperated sigh and stood. "This isn't getting us anywhere."

"Oh, my God, probably the tide has come in and washed it out to sea!" Her hand flew to her mouth.

"Were you near the water?"

"I was near the edge of the marsh grass when the Phantom appeared. Do you think there's a chance…?"

"High tide was at midnight yesterday. It can rise into the grass. Believe me, I know. I've gotten my feet wet often enough as a result. Let's go and see what we can find."

"You're on."

****

They headed down the beach. They hadn't gone far when Danielle, walking slightly ahead of Andrew and Aladdin, stopped.

"It's gone!" The two words gasped from her lips. She broke into a run down the beach, desperate to discover that either the wind or the tide had knocked it from sight. When she reached the spot, she found nothing but three holes in the sand where she'd planted the tripod legs. The ground was dry…no tide had washed it away, and the tripod wasn't lying on its side, as a high wind would have left it.

"No sign of it at all?" Andrew came to join her.

"No, it's not here, neither camera nor tripod, only three marks left by its legs in the sand." Cold, hard fear knotted in her gut. "And there are no footprints leading to or away from the spot."

"Oh, come on. There must be. Some kids out for a moonlight sail must have spotted it and decided to take it. It would have looked abandoned."

"No, no, no! No footprints anywhere."

"Well, it would be easy enough to expunge them with a broom made of marsh grass."

"But you and I are the only people on this island! Unless…"

"Unless what?"

"Unless the ghost decided to come back. Maybe he was afraid I'd managed to take his photo."

"Come on, Dani. A three-hundred-year-old phantom worried about his image being caught on a digital camera? Think about it. My theory about kids out for a sail makes a whole lot more sense. Anyhow, you can use your backup camera and try again tonight."

"I don't have a backup camera." The moment the words were out of her mouth, she realized the hole they'd make in her fake identity.

"You don't?" He faced her, incredulity written over his features.

"No, I don't. It was stolen on my way here, when I

went into a convenience store for a soft drink and forgot to lock the car doors."

"And they didn't take the other camera?"

"I must have come out of the store before they had time." *Please stop facing me with the disbelieving expression all over you.* "Anyhow, the other camera was new, still in the box. A much better one to steal."

"Did you report it to the police?"

"No. I didn't want to take the time. I was anxious to make the trip here in a single day. Motels cost big money, you know." Cold sweat trickled down between her breasts. *Stop questioning me. Just stop.*

"Well, then, may I suggest we take a trip to the mainland? To New Harbor, the town that boasts the new fish processing plant that all but closed Cavalier's Cove down." He drew in a deep breath, raising his broad shoulders. "There's a nice little photography shop in the center of town. Wade told me about it."

"No!"

"What? For God's sake, why not? Without a camera, there's no reason for you to stay on the island." He faced her, exasperation obvious in his tone and expression. "Does that mean you're planning to leave?"

"No. That is… I don't know."

"Well, you'll have to decide. Call me on the CB when you make up your mind." He turned away and grasped the dog's leash. "Home, Aladdin."

"No, wait!" He'd only gone a few steps before she ran after him and grasped his arm. "No, I don't plan to leave the island." Her tone moderated as he turned back to her. "And I'd be grateful if you'd take me to that photography shop."

He hesitated. She held her breath.

"All right." He smiled. His response released the lump of tension in her gut. "I'll call Wade on the CB as soon as I get home and ask him to send Jimmy out around ten a.m. That okay with you?"

"Sure, okay, fine." She released his arm and stepped back from him. "I'll pick you up at your house."

"Good." He started back toward his house. "See you shortly."

****

I have to be crazy, going into a town after Harry explicitly told me to stay here. But how could I refuse? If I'm supposed to be a photographer on the island to try to get a picture of a ghost, I won't have a reason to stay if I don't have a camera. Damn, damn, damn.

She applied more tanning lotion to her face, hands, and arms, and sat down on the couch with Bibsy to wait for it to dry.

"On a positive note, Bibsy"—she stroked the little cat—"with this short, dark hair and California Girl tan, accompanied by a blind man and a wolf dog, I doubt if my parents or my brother would recognize me." She stood and strode into the bedroom to peer at herself in the crazed mirror. The warmth of the morning was fading into chilly overcast.

Damn, I look tacky. I need a change of clothes, but I haven't anything else even remotely warm enough for another dark, cold day.

She went to the bathroom and turned on the shower. Back in the bedroom, she dug shampoo, conditioner, and body wash from her cosmetic case. Shucking her wrinkled outfit as she went, she returned to the bathroom. With a sigh, she stepped into the warm, reviving flow.

At least I won't have to be guilty of smelling bad. That should be a major sensory issue with a visually challenged—excuse me, blind—person.

****

He was waiting in his weedy, overgrown dooryard when she arrived shortly before ten o'clock. He'd topped jeans with a tan sweater and brown leather jacket.

Damn, but the man is eye candy. Wonder how he chooses his clothes…must be by touch.

"Have you been waiting long?" She got out of the car to direct him to the passenger side and let Aladdin into the back.

"Not long. It'll be good to get off the island for a while."

"Understandable." She watched him settle into the passenger side and grope for the seatbelt. "Here, let me help…although I doubt you'll need it unless our horseman blocks the path."

The last reeked of sarcasm as she bent into the car to reach across him to find the seatbelt. Her breast encountered his chest, her hand his hip, and something shot through her with hot intensity.

In a rush she snapped the belt in place and lurched back, bumping her head on the roof as she exited.

"Ouch!"

"Bumped your head?" He interpreted the sound. "Am I that repulsive that you have to leap away from me?"

"No…oh, no." Suddenly conscious of how the man must feel after his accident, she hurried to compensate. "I…"

"It's okay. Not a whole lot of sex appeal in a lame blind man."

"That's not it…not it at all…"

"Can we go now? Jimmy will be waiting." He faced stubbornly forward, his features grim, his jaw working with a tick.

"Of course." She closed his door and went around to the driver's side.

If only he knew the truth. If only he knew how absolutely attractive—not to mention downright sexy—he is. …to me.

****

At the camera shop in the bustling waterfront town of New Harbor with its massive state-of-the-art fish processing plant dominating one end of the main street, she bought a camera and tripod with the cash Harry had provided. *No plastic when making purchases. Don't leave a trail of any kind.* His warning echoed back to her.

"Not a really high-end bit of equipment for a professional photographer," Andrew Drack remarked as they left the shop.

"How would you know?" Nervousness made her snap with a cruelty she regretted instantly. "Andrew, I shouldn't have said…"

"I heard the sales clerk give you the total of your purchases." He stopped on the street outside the shop and swung on her. "I'm blind, not deaf."

"Oh, God, don't let's fight." She took his arm, and with her on one side and the dog on the other, they started back toward her car, the packages clutched to her chest. "Things haven't been going all that well for me, either. First, that dilapidated cottage on a spooky island, then that being on the horse, which you don't believe in, and finally, but not least importantly, my career in tatters…"

He stopped short and turned to her. "Sorry. I'm truly sorry."

They stood facing each other in the nearly deserted parking lot in the dismal day, silence hanging between them.

"I thought we banished that word." She drew a deep breath and forced her tone to lighten.

"On the island. Here, I'm free to apologize any way I choose. And I will. I'm taking you to lunch at one of the best little seafood restaurants anywhere on the coast."

"No, Andrew, really, that isn't necessary."

"Oh, but I think it is. Furthermore, I'd enjoy a meal I didn't fumble around to fix or bum off of you. It should be four or five stores down from the camera shop. It's built right out over the water…great atmosphere. Think you can find it?"

"Sure. Thanks. Set Aladdin in motion, and we're off."

****

This is the best lobster I've ever eaten.

An hour later Danielle placed her napkin beside her plate and uttered a contented sigh. *And in just about the best company.* She looked over at Andrew. He'd apparently put bitterness and suspicion aside and devoted himself to her enjoyment. They had talked about favorite music, books, and even movies he'd seen before the accident. She had discovered they had a lot in common. His affable interest, devoid of annoyance and discontent, had been what she needed after time spent on that eerie scrap of dislocated land.

"We'd better be getting back," she said finally, struggling to keep regret out of her words. The idea of returning to the island brought a sick feeling washing over her.

"Dessert? They make a wonderful strawberry shortcake." He smiled, and she hesitated, wanting to say yes, wanting to prolong their time together.

No, no, no. I have to get back to the island before something goes wrong, before someone recognizes me.

"Tempting, but no, thank you. I couldn't manage another bit. Anyhow, strawberries are out of season." She stood, making sure her chair made enough noise to indicate her movement.

"If you're sure." He got to his feet. "Come on, boy," he said to the dog lying under the table. "Maybe we should go before the staff starts questioning that side order of hamburger. Service dogs may be allowed in here, but I don't think they're supposed to order from the menu."

As he gathered up the handle of the dog's harness, he smiled in Danielle's direction, a smile that sent a tingle over her senses.

Damn, damn, damn.

****

They were waiting for Jimmy Waters at the wharf when a RCMP cruiser drove out onto the wharf and stopped beside them. Danielle experienced the all-too-familiar lurch of fear as its door opened and Constable Wade James emerged. When he headed for their car, her heart began to pound.

"Good afternoon, Miss Breckenreid." He leaned toward her window, and she had little choice but to wind it down. "I'm assuming it is Miss Breckenreid?"

"Yes. What can we do for you, Officer?"

"Wade?" She caught a note of astonishment in Andrew's query. "Didn't expect to meet you here."

"Yes, well, I'm just getting back to Cavalier's Cove. Tanker truck rolled on the highway about ten miles west of here. All emergency personnel in the area were called to respond."

"An unexpected development." Andrew wet his lips and shifted in his seat.

"Definitely. Well, that's the nature of the job, isn't it. You never know what's going to happen next." He gave the roof of the car a slap as he straightened up. "Now I'd better be getting back to the office."

"Good afternoon, Constable. I hope the rest of your day is peaceful." Danielle fought to remain casually friendly.

"I'm counting on it, Miss Breckenreid. I haven't had lunch, and I don't enjoy missing meals."

After he'd gotten back into his cruiser and driven away, Danielle turned to her passenger.

"Constable James appears to be a nice man," she said as Jimmy Waters hobbled onto the wharf behind them.

"What? Oh, yes, he is…a nice man, that is."

****

"Will you come to dinner at my house this evening? You can bring Bibsy. I'll guarantee Aladdin will be a perfect gentleman." He'd limped around to her door after getting out of the vehicle at the doorstep of his farmhouse.

"Andrew, we've just had lunch together."

"And I enjoyed it very much. So much so I want to

74

have the pleasure of your company at another meal."

Danielle hesitated. While she didn't welcome the idea of spending another evening alone in the creepy old cottage, she couldn't help but wonder if it would be wise to spend one with this man who seemed to be possessed of two personas. But he was handsome and charming and charismatic...

Her spirit of adventure kicked in. "Sure, why not. Night life on this island appears to be more than a tad limited. "Did I hear you invite Bibsy? Is she to be a guest or your friend's main course?"

"Hardly." He grinned around the glasses. "I thought you'd feel more secure if you brought a friend."

"I appreciate the thought, but I'll leave her home."

"Can't fully bring yourself to trust your pet with mine, is that it? Understandable, I guess. Wade tells me he looks like a timber wolf." He paused to stroke the dog's head.

"Actually, he's very handsome," she said, struck by a wave of sadness for this man who'd never seen his trusted companion. "Variegated shades of gray and white—silver, really—with mesmerizing golden eyes that have an almost surreal look to them."

"Just what this place needs. Another spook."

"I meant it as a compliment."

"Sure you did." She caught the humor in his tone and saw his mouth quirk up at a corner. "Six o'clock, then." He felt his jacket pockets. "Where did I put my keys?"

"You locked your house, after you've done all you can to convince me there are only four of us on the island and today all of us but Bibsy were on the mainland?"

"Hey, look, someone stole your tripod and camera. This island isn't completely isolated. People in boats can reach it, no problem."

"I suppose." She started to get out of the car. "I'll help you look. Maybe you dropped them after you locked up."

"No need." He pulled them out. "Just deep pockets."

"Do you need me to see you inside?"

"Hardly." Again the bitterness. "I've gotten myself in and out well enough before you arrived."

"Okay, okay. Geez. Hope you're not so touchy tonight. See you later."

Danielle shifted into drive, turned in the weedy dooryard, and headed back down the road.

Chapter Five

"No, no, no!"

Danielle discarded one outfit after another. What to wear to dinner at Andrew's was becoming a major problem. She paused in sorting through the clothes in her suitcase. Intended for a romantic weekend in Montreal, none appeared suitable. Spaghetti-strap tops, short hip-hugging skirts, and stiletto heels had no place in the cold autumn chill of Phantom Island, never mind the sexy nighties and underwear.

"I know what you're thinking," she sighed, sinking down beside the cat curled up on the bed. "This is crazy. The man is blind. But it's late October and I don't want to freeze. I doubt that mausoleum he lives in has central heating."

She chose tan dress pants and matched them with a soft tangerine-colored sweater, the closest outfit to appropriate for a chilly autumn evening.

"What do you think?" She held her choice up for Bibsy.

The cat muttered something in her throat.

"Okay, okay, I'm not trying to impress the man. Really. I know there can't ever be anything between us. I'm not who he thinks I am, and, if he ever finds out, I wouldn't blame him for putting as much space between us as possible. Furthermore, he hasn't given me any reason to believe he wants anything more than friendship. Who knows, he may already have a significant other." She stared down at the cat, her eyes widening as the thought washed over her mind. "He may even be married!"

"No, he isn't," she contradicted herself. "He's not wearing a wedding ring. Most men do these days, and he's the type who would...I think."

She paused in front of the crazed mirror above the dresser, her lower lip sucked in, the sweater clutched to her chest. Her hair was all wrong. Neither the color nor the new coiffure suited her. *Damn!*

She dropped the garment to pick up a brush and run it through her abbreviated style. It didn't help. She just plain didn't like it. But, then, she shouldn't complain. Cutting her hair and changing its color had been a small price to pay for freedom. If Andrew Drack weren't providing a bit of distraction, she'd be a ball of terrified worry. And what good would that do?

The pants needed pressing. She carried them into the kitchen and lowered the old wooden ironing board on its wall hanging.

She found a vintage electric iron in a cupboard above the washer but paused as she was about to plug it into an outlet. A bare wire lay exposed halfway along the length of the cord. She sighed and replaced the iron in its cupboard. No need to risk electrocuting herself. On an inspiration, she began to search the kitchen drawers for electrical tape.

Hester Matthew had amassed a vast collection of junk that ranged from rusted nutcrackers to doughnut cutters with the center hole section missing, but no electrical tape. Heading back into the bedroom to dress, she shrugged. So what. She'd go to dinner a bit wrinkled. Andrew wouldn't know.

****

By the time she was ready to leave, the temperature had dropped several degrees. When she stepped out onto the veranda, the ocean lay in a dead calm. A nasty chill had settled over the island.

She turned up the collar of her jacket and shivered. There'd be frost before dawn. Soon ice would crust that benign-looking water…ice not thick enough to allow passage on its surface, but making it impossible for Jimmy Waters to come, even to bring supplies. She'd be trapped.

Another shiver washed over her. The thin summer jacket she wore wouldn't do. By the time she'd be returning to the cottage later in the evening, the temperature would probably be even lower. She remembered an old sheepskin-lined jacket she'd seen hanging on a peg by the kitchen door. Hester's, no doubt. While she didn't fancy wearing the dead woman's clothing, she was even less willing to be miserably cold. She turned back into the cottage.

Bibsy yowled at her return, and she grinned.

"Playing watch cat? Good."

She snatched the old jacket from its peg near the kitchen door, gave it a sharp shake to free it of dust and (heaven forbid) any spiders that might be lurking inside. With a grimace, she thrust her arms into the sleeve and waited a moment, to see if anything crawled over her, before buttoning it.

As she started once more for the door, a thought struck her. *Wine. I should take a bottle of wine. I am a dinner guest, and it would be appropriate.*

She went to the cupboard and selected the most

expensive of those she'd purchased at the convenience store where she'd stocked up on supplies.

"Good night again, Bibsy," she called to the cat as she went out and turned the key. Andrew's explanation for locking his farmhouse had made her cautious.

Heading once more up the beach, she thrust her hands deep into the pockets of the old coat. Her fingers encountered something smooth and rectangular. Paper. Smooth paper. A photograph. Pausing, she pulled it out. And gasped.

It was an image of a man in a flowing cape and wide-brimmed hat, mounted on a horse that reared against the face of a full moon. Hester Matthews had managed to get a photo of the horseman!

Shoving it back into the pocket where she'd found it, her heart pounding, she set off at a run toward Andrew's house.

Proof, proof! Now I have proof that the horseman exists.

Chapter Six

The discovery was still sending thrills of excitement dancing over her as she paused to catch her breath at the foot of the decrepit wooden steps leading up the crumbling sandstone bank to Andrew's weatherbeaten farmhouse. She couldn't wait to tell him about it. Then another thought struck.

He can't see it. He might think we should call in his Mountie friend to verify what I describe to him. I don't want that...not at all. The less I have to do with Constable Wade James, the better. Anyhow, the photo belonged to Hester Matthews. I'll save it for Harry. It's rightfully part of his inheritance. He can decide what we should do with it.

She shoved the photo deeper into her pocket, drew a deep breath, and headed up the steps.

Really, this place does look like something out of a horror movie. She paused at the top of the incline to gaze at the dilapidated structure. *I must have been mad to accept his invitation. I'll go back to the cottage and call him on the CB, tell him I'm not feeling well...*

As she turned to retreat to the beach, a barrage of barking stopped her.

"Good evening." Andrew Drack's voice made her whirl. He'd opened the door and stood framed against the house's darkened interior, a smile on his lips. He was dressed entirely in black...black silk shirt, well-

81

fitted black pants, a darkly handsome figure veiled in an ambience of mystery that upped her heartbeats in the chill October twilight.

"Sorry about the hostile greeting," he continued, with the dog now silent, standing at his side. "In spite of his surreal eyes, he can't see through doors, but he does have acute hearing. Aladdin, apologize and make Dani welcome."

The dog hesitated and then, tail wagging slowly, ambled forward. Danielle stood her ground but couldn't quite relax. Something in those tawny eyes reeked of mistrust, of being ready to attack at a moment's notice.

"Extend your hand, let him smell it. I want you two to be friends. Did you bring Bibsy?"

"No...no." Danielle held her breath as a long, pink tongue lapped over her fingers. "I thought that might be pu...pushing the envelope."

"Maybe so." Andrew leaned against the doorframe. "Anyway, you two are going to be just fine. Unless I'm badly mistaken, my boy has played the gallant and kissed your hand. That means you're accepted, not that he's conducting a taste test."

"That's a relief." Danielle stroked the animal's soft silver head.

"Come in, Dani. You must be cold. I have a fire in the living room." He extended a hand.

She hesitated. *Get smart, Danielle. Get the hell out of here while you still can. This man is way too charming, too smooth, too perfect, too, too draculian...if there is such a word.*

"Dani?" Her name was a soft, seductive question. She found her fingers encased in his, his grasp sending a cornucopia of feelings flooding from the point of contact through her entire body. Entranced, she let him draw her into the house.

The light scent of his aftershave wafted over her as she passed close in front of him to enter the house. Something sophisticated and expensive. What had Andrew Drack been before he'd hermited himself away on Phantom Island? Male model? Millionaire? Master criminal? James Bond type of spy? More to the point, how did he manage to shave and not be covered with nicks or rash?

"You must find shaving difficult." The words blurted out.

"At first I did." A corner of his mouth quirked. "According to Wade, I looked as if I'd been through a skirmish with an irritated cat. But I learned, adjusted. Why? Do I have a series of unsightly nicks?"

"No, no, not at all. You've done a fine job...not a single scratch or cut."

I'm bumbling. Get a grip, Danielle.

Another thought struck her. He spoke of the RCMP officer often and with familiarity. Had Andrew Drack been a lawman before the accident? Was that why Constable Wade James acted as Andrew Drack's caretaker? Didn't those guys stick together, no matter what? *My luck couldn't possibly be that bad. Oh, good lord, will you look at this!*

The foyer she'd entered was the essence of Victorian gloom. Lined with mahogany, it opened into a vestibule with a dark staircase that led upwards to disappear around a shadowy bend. To her right, an arch gave way to a heavily bric-a-bracked, overly furnished Victorian parlor. Dark red wallpaper embossed with a baroque design hung faded and peeling on the walls.

The hand-carved wooden trim of the nineteenth-century furniture was scratched and chipped, its upholstery threadbare. A once-garish red-and-green area rug grown thin and dull covered the center of the foot-weary oak floor. A massive bow window that opened out toward the bay was so heavily hung with faded maroon draperies and yellowed lace undercurtains it allowed little of the last light of day to penetrate.

Dracula would have felt right at home in this creepy old place. And Andrew Drack is handsome, charming, mysterious... Oh, come on. Don't get crazy. There're no such things as vampires. It's just the appearance of this spooky old place that's making you think insane thoughts.

"Please. Sit down. Here, by the fire." Andrew's alacrity stopped her imaginings and drew her attention to the only cheerful note in the dismal room, a fire crackling on a stone hearth at the far wall. "Do you have a jacket or coat? May I take it?"

See? He's simply a nice man, probably more than a little lonely. Anyhow, I've never heard of any blind, lame vampires.

"Thanks." She shrugged out of her jacket and handed it to him with one hand, putting the wine in his other. "I brought wine." When she caught a hint of apprehension in his expression, she continued, "I promise not to overindulge." She hoped he caught the humor her words.

"I'll see to it. Aladdin and I plan to walk, not carry, you home later." *Ah, good, he had.* "Care to read the label for me?"

"My French is faulty." She proceeded to spell the name.

Turning the bottle over in his hands, he translated in what she heard as flawless French. *Yet another mysterious part of the man's character.*

"You must do well as a photographer to be able to buy in this price range."

"It was a gift…from a friend." Yet another lie. She couldn't tell him she'd been so unnerved she'd simply grabbed several bottles at random off the shelves in the liquor outlet attached to the convenience store where she'd bought her groceries.

"A man?" He raised an eyebrow above his glasses.

"As a matter of fact, yes. When I decided to come to Phantom Island, he gave me a few bottles…in case the place started to get to me."

"Which it obviously has at least once." He returned to the vestibule to hang her jacket in a dark closet under the stairs. She glimpsed a pile of what appeared to be small valises stacked inside before he shut the door. "This friend. Serious?"

"Could be." *Why not let him think I'm capable of attracting a man? And it could be serious with Harry.*

"Ah-ha. So nothing definite…yet."

"Not yet."

"But you have hopes?"

"You're making it sound like something out of a regency novel. No, I simply find him intriguing. Andrew, are you French?"

"French father, English mother. What makes you ask?"

"You were so fluent in pronouncing the name on that bottle of wine."

"Gave myself away. But don't get any fantasies about me. I'm not like the dashing Frenchman of du

Maurier fame. I'm hardly in any condition to sweep you off on a romantic adventure aboard my pirate ship."

"I wouldn't want you to. The discomforts aboard one of those vessels aren't for me." *Teasing now, making light of his handicap. I can handle this.*

"Tonight you don't have to worry." He paused and smiled in the direction of her voice. "Tonight you can have me for as long as you choose." The last sentence held a husky innuendo.

Oh, God, those damned butterflies again. Get back to joking around…quickly.

"Was that a come-on?"

"Oh, damn. I said that all wrong. I only meant…"

"Really?"

"Okay, okay. It must have sounded pretty ridiculous if you took it as such. A blind, lame guy hitting on a successful, probably beautiful photographer." He let the corner of his mouth quirk in what Danielle could only interpret as a rueful apology.

"So if we hadn't banished a certain five-letter word, you'd probably be using it right now?"

"Yeah, possibly."

"Okay, moving on."

"Fine." He held up the wine. "I'll decant this. After Aladdin's greeting, I'm sure you'd like to wash up before dinner. The bathroom is at the top of the stairs, to the left. Wade tells me it appears to have been converted from a closet or storeroom. The point is, there's no window. You'll have to turn on the light before you let the door close. The switch is to the right, inside."

"Thanks." *No window, a closet. What a delightful collection of buzzwords for someone with my phobia.*

As she made her way up the stairs into the shadows and rounded the dark curve near the top, her heartbeat quickened, her steps slowed. Scenes from every vintage horror movie she'd ever seen began to crowd into her mind. She half expected some of those bats he'd mentioned as inhabiting the island to flutter into her face.

They didn't. She reached the top to see a long, dark corridor with peeling wallpaper and threadbare carpeting stretching the full length of the house in front of her. Several closed doors lined its shadowy length, including one to her immediate left.

She pulled it open.

The room revealed was as black as pitch. The ugly, familiar sensations of shortness of breath, nausea, sweating, and madly racing heart overwhelmed her. She released the knob, and the door, responding to the cant of the old house, swung shut.

She stood panting, her hand clutched to her throat. *This is ridiculous. It's only a dark room. Once I find the light switch, I'll be fine.*

Anyhow, she couldn't go back downstairs without using the wash basin. He'd notice if no water had trickled down through the pipes. He'd wonder why she hadn't washed her hands. He might even ask. She couldn't risk explaining that a devil-may-care photographer like Dani Breckenreid was a raging claustrophobic.

She grasped the knob for a second time. *Stop wimping out. I have to wash my hands before dinner. Aladdin made that essential. One, two, three—here goes.* She pulled open the door and, heart thudding, fumbled along the wall inside for the light switch.

The moment she flicked it on and the room was flooded with light, her fears relaxed. From its claw-footed tub to its wall-hung washbasin and the toilet with an antiquated ceiling-high flushing system, the room was simply a 1920s attempt at bringing twentieth-century plumbing to a nineteenth-century house. No attempt had been made at decoration. Purely functional, its walls consisted of cracked, shedding plaster, its floor covered with broken linoleum exuding the musty smell of damp and possibly rotting floorboards beneath.

On the positive side, thick white towels on a bar between the tub and washbasin appeared fresh and clean. Above the sink, on a narrow shelf, an assortment of male grooming products had been assembled. A cracked and crazed mirror completed the accoutrements.

She turned on a tap at the washbasin. Water spouted out in bursts and gasps. It splashed over the front of her sweater, and she jumped back, grabbing a towel to brush it off before it penetrated.

By the time she'd finished, the old plumbing had settled down. A steady if slim stream of water issued from the tap. She picked up a bar of soap and rubbed it over her wet hands.

As she rinsed away the lather, her peripheral vision caught the door again moving in sympathy with the slant of the house. *No!* She lunged but was too late. It shut with a bump. A sharp click followed as a lock fell into place. The light winked and went out.

Too stunned to react, she stood frozen in place. *Oh, God, oh, God, oh, God!*

She stumbled to the door, grabbed the knob, and wrenched.

Stuck, locked! I'm trapped!

She banged on the panel, clawed it, tried to scream, but there wasn't enough air. Panting, her lungs clamoring for oxygen by the time Andrew yanked the door open, she fell into his arms and passed out.

****

When she returned to consciousness, she discovered she was lying on a four-poster bed covered with a frayed patchwork quilt. A sleeping bag with a single pillow stacked on top was folded beside her.

"What…?"

She tried to sit up, the damp facecloth that had been on her forehead sliding away. In the deepening twilight, Andrew, seated beside her, pushed her back gently.

"Rest." His voice sensuously soft, he looked darkly, seductively handsome. She'd never understood why women could be charmed by a vampire, but she was beginning to get the idea.

"Claustrophobia?" He replaced the cool cloth, letting his fingers linger lightly on her cheek.

"Yes." The word was a wheezed sigh of resignation. Denying it would be ridiculous.

"What happened? Were you trapped somewhere as a child?" His words, smooth as silk, reassured her, made her willing to trust this strange, dark man in the bewitching shadows of the old bedroom…at least for the moment.

"Yes." She closed her eyes and struggled to repress the shudder the memory always sent coursing through her. "We were at my grandparents' farm. I was five years old. I wandered away and fell through the rotted boards of an old well. Fortunately it had gone dry, but I was trapped down that awful hole overnight before they found me. It was cold and dark, and there were rustling, slithering sounds, and I couldn't...couldn't...get out...no matter how I clawed at those walls...and I couldn't breathe!"

She bolted upright, a familiar cold sweat pouring over her body.

"Easy, easy." He took her into his arms. Exhausted, she slumped, ragdoll-like, against him.

"That's better." He stroked her hair. "Relax. Phobias can be pretty awful. I should know. I used to have a fear of flying that was second to none."

"In an airplane?" She pulled out from him and looked up into his face.

Oh, damn, where did that come from?

"Of course, in an airplane." A frown furrowing his forehead. "How else?"

"I don't know." She tried to shrug it off. "Hang glider, dirigible, hot air balloon..."

"Magic powers? Look, I'm not a warlock. Is this house so bad you're seeing me as some kind of spirit of the night?" She caught teasing humor in his tone.

"No, no, that is..."

Again that deep, throaty, thrilling chuckle.

"A blind, lame vampire? Wouldn't I make an original in a horror story? Maybe I'm only blind and lame in daylight. Maybe at night I can see, and glide through the air..."

"Stop. You're making fun of me simply because I have an active imagination."

"Active? I'd say super-active. If I didn't think I'd be embarrassing you, I'd tell Wade. He'd have one huge belly laugh. He's always thought of me as dull and insipid."

So I won't worry about Constable Wade James. Anyone who sees this guy as dull and insipid can't be all that bright.

"I'd prefer you didn't." She shrugged away from him and swung her legs over the edge of the bed. *Better to put some distance between us.* "Would you like to tell me about your fear of flying…in an airplane?"

"Sure. Unlike you, I have absolutely no idea what caused it. Contrary to what you may have imagined, my mother wasn't a witch who dropped me as an infant while she was whisking through the air on her broom." His mouth tilted into a half grin. "The important thing is I discovered a way to deal with it. These days I can take a commercial aircraft and not dissolve into a nauseated, suffocating mass."

"How?" She stared up at him as if he'd just told her he could perform miracles.

"Exposure therapy. It consists of gradually exposing yourself in small but ever increasing amounts to the thing you fear. I did it, and it was working. In the final stages, I got a powerful motivation to overcome it real fast."

"Which was?"

"I was in Nova Scotia when I got the news that my father had suffered a heart attack in British Columbia. He's fine now, but at the time the doctors didn't think he'd make it. I had to get there fast. So I forced myself aboard an Air Canada flight and managed to get to Vancouver without forcing the pilot to land because of a meltdown."

"So you're saying I should lock myself away in the dark? Never!"

"Not just like that." He touched her cheek with his fingertips. "I'm not sure of the procedure for treating claustrophobia, but assuming it runs a parallel to my experience, I'd say you'd start simply by going into a small, windowless room with a trusted friend, lights on, door open. After you become reasonably comfortable with that scenario, you try it with the door closed. Then, alone. Eventually, the light could be put out and you could still manage to feel reasonably in control, or at least not panicked to the point of irrational desperation."

"I…don't know…"

"I'll help you, if you like. We could try it together."

"No! I won't go back into that room. Not now. Not ever!" She lurched to her feet, eyes wild with terror.

"I'm not suggesting we start this minute." He got up to stand in front of her. "I meant some time when you're calm and happy, when *you're* ready. Agreed?"

"I'll consider it." She decided to change the subject. "This is your bedroom?" She looked about at the tattered wallpaper, the bare plank floor, the scratched dresser and chipped armoire, ragged bed, and the rolled-up sleeping bag.

"Yes." He grinned ruefully. "Pretty grim, Wade told me, yet he said it's the most livable one in the house. I've been toying with the idea of investing in some better bedding, but a sleeping bag and pillow seem to be all I need…at least right now."

"Now *that* was a come on if I ever heard one." Danielle felt her spirits lifting.

"I guess it was." In the moonlight beginning to enter the room, she could make out his grin. "I must be

92

getting my confidence back. I may even get up to being incredibly romantic this evening."

"Really? What if I'm not so inclined?"

"Then we'll take that into consideration and proceed at your pleasure. But first"—his lightened tone returned—"hand washing. I'll stand in the bathroom doorway so this crooked old house won't continue to play tricks on you, okay?"

"I think I left the tap running. Sorry."

"Not to worry. The old place has an excellent deep water well and a fine drainage system. We're not about to be flooded out or end up dry."

"Nevertheless, we should check." She struggled to make an argument that would force her to return to that awful bathroom, to face her fears with him by her side. It would be a start...if what he'd told her about overcoming her phobia was true.

"Yes, we should." His words, soft in the moonlight, told her he understood.

"Okay, then, off we go." She sucked in a deep breath. "My hands feel a bit sticky with the soap I didn't finish rinsing off."

When he swept out an arm for her to precede him, she managed to walk out of the room and down the hall.

"The light went out, too," she said.

"Maybe the bulb is loose," he replied as they reached the bathroom. "When the door slammed, it probably disconnected. Direct me to it. I'll check."

"Not necessary. I'm capable of screwing in a light bulb."

"An independent woman." He swept her a mocking bow. "Go ahead. I'll guard the door."

She hesitated before stepping into the dark room.

Suppressing a shudder, she reached up and tightened the bulb. The small, dingy room flooded with light.

"Done." The word came out sounding more like a sigh of relief than she'd wanted it to.

"Ah-ha. First step. You're already on the road to recovery."

She went to the basin and rinsed the last of the soap from her hands.

****

"Sit here, please." He held out a chair for her at a long mahogany table in the gloomy nineteenth-century dining room on the ground floor. "I've set two places at one corner. It's such a massive thing I didn't want us to spend the evening shouting at each other up and down its length. I hope you don't mind being denied the place of honor at the far end."

"I'd feel lonely way down there." She looked along the length of the table in the shadowy moonlight casting rays through the window at the far end.

"Good." He adjusted her chair as she sat down. "Excuse me. I'll check on dinner."

Apparently confident in his own house, he exited the room without a trace of uncertainty. After he'd gone, she studied the scarred oak table neatly set at one corner for two. A pair of tall, unlit, snow-white candles in tarnished silver holders had been placed between the two settings. She wished he'd remembered to light them. She didn't like the eeriness of this strange old house with night gliding over it.

Andrew returned carrying a well-filled salad bowl and a basket of crusty garlic bread. She relaxed and smiled at him.

"I'll get the lasagna," he said. He returned to the

kitchen and shortly was back with a casserole and a decanter filled with the wine she'd brought. "The lasagna and garlic bread are the freezer variety, I'm afraid."

Danielle caught the uncertainty in his tone and wondered if this was the first time he'd invited a woman to dinner since his accident. On the chance that it was, it wouldn't be appropriate to mention the unlighted candles.

"It looks wonderful," she replied. "How did you know lasagna is my favorite meal? After lobster, of course."

"Maybe my intuition is one of those senses they say is sharpened when you lose another." He sat down at the head of the table, picked up the salad bowl, and offered it to her. "I can't say the same for my salad-making ability. Let me know if you find anything in this that isn't a vegetable."

"I'm not worried," she said taking up the tongs. "You haven't made a single mistake since I've known you."

"Really? So why are we sitting down to dinner with unlit candles?" Bitterness suddenly colored his tone. He leaned forward and ran his hand over the table's surface until he found a book of matches. "Do you mind?" He held them out to her. "I don't want to chance setting the house on fire."

"Of course not." She struck one and held it to first one candle, then the other. Their wicks wavered to life, casting seductive shadows around the room.

"I should have lighted them the moment you knocked on the door, to establish the ambience, yet they would still have had enough life left to last...until they weren't needed." His voice softened seductively over the last sentence.

"You sound experienced at setting up candlelit dinners." Something she hated to admit might be jealousy nipped at her. "Right down to timing their length."

"Maybe...once upon a time. Wine?" His fingers closed around the decanter, but not before Danielle saw a slight tremor in them. Reaching out, she covered them with her hand.

He released the container, caught her fingers in his, and brought her hand, palm upwards to his lips in a gesture so spontaneous, so sexually titillating in the flickering candlelight it sent a surge of something hot and erotic coursing down her body.

"Andrew." His name gasped from her lips.

As if burned, he dropped her hand. Bumping the table, he stumbled to his feet and in two strides was at the window. His back to her, he faced out into the dark, brooding spruce trees that pushed like claws against its panes.

The room fell silent except for the crackle of the parlor fire and the ticking of a grandfather clock in a far corner. And the hammering of Danielle's heart.

When he turned back to her, his features were grim in the heavy veil of shadows.

"That was a stupid move," he said.

"It was lovely...romantic. But maybe, at least for now, we should remain just friends."

"Yeah, right. Friends." His shoulders rose and fell in a shrug of acceptance.

He returned to the table and immediately launched into a line of conversation Danielle guessed he was struggling to keep within the acceptable area of two people getting to know each other. He talked about how he was becoming accustomed to audio books and told her amusing anecdotes about his adjusting to trusting Aladdin. He had an interest in anthropology, and they fell into a discussion until Danielle feared she might be giving away her real profession by being too knowledgeable. She paused, allowing a gap in the conversation.

"Will you pour more wine?" He held up his glass.

"Of course." She refreshed first his drink and, after a pause, shrugged and did hers as well. She was enjoying the evening.

"But you know what really fascinates me?" he said as she replaced the bottle on the table.

"Tell me."

"Egyptology. Whenever I was near a major museum that had any kind of display, I headed right for it. What about you? Are you interested in the days of the pharaohs?"

"Not really." Tightness suffused her chest. *God, don't let me have a heart attack. His interest is happenstance, nothing more, nothing more.* "It's getting late. I should be going."

"We haven't had our coffee. Let the unlit candles be my biggest faux pas of the evening. Don't cause me to make another by permitting a guest to leave without coffee."

He let the subject drop as casually as he'd introduced it. He stood and headed for the kitchen. Relief surged through her.

"Let me help."

"No, of course not. You're my guest. Go into the

parlor and sit by the fire. I'll be back shortly. Aladdin will keep you company. He's already in there, snoozing on the rug in front of the hearth."

****

Danielle settled on the old sofa and watched the flames dancing, providing the only illumination in the dark Victorian room. Once again she thought it to be the perfect setting for a gothic novel, complete with a dark, handsome, mysterious man to provide romance.

"Ready for coffee and brandy?" Startling her with his seemingly silent approach, he came into the room. He carried a tray with two cups, a decanter, and two brandy glasses.

"Brandy?" She looked up at him as he set it on the table in front of her. "After wine with dinner…"

"You're not driving. Aladdin and I will be walking you home."

Her arguments stilled, Danielle watched as he poured them each a measure before sitting down beside her.

****

"Let me touch your face," he said softly.

"What?"

They'd finished their coffee and brandy and had been sitting on the sofa, facing the dying fire in what Danielle had considered companionable silence. Until this.

"I want to know if you're as beautiful as I've imagined." The last sentence, rich with seductive innuendo, sent a quiver of excitement coursing through her.

She hesitated. In her chest, something like the frantic beating of eagles' wings had begun. Her mind scrambled for a reason to refuse. None came. Body and spirit both longed to allow him.

"Yes," she whispered.

As his fingers traced her features, his touch as sensual as a lover's, her body tingled, glowed, and ignited with heated longing.

Oh, God, now I truly understand women's desire to surrender to handsome vampires. I have to get away! Now!

She pulled back, her breathing ragged.

Good God, what's happening? I've never felt anything like that with any other man.

"Dani, are you okay?" His face creased with lines of concern.

"Yes, fine. What's the verdict?" She struggled to sound flip and teasing. "In your opinion, am I absolutely gorgeous, maybe beautiful, simply pretty, or a hopeless hag?"

"Midway." He drew back, a corner of his mouth curled up in what she saw as a sardonic grin. "But I'm leaning toward the gorgeous side."

"Ah, well, now, there it is. Definite proof of your ancestry."

"What do you mean?"

"Irish, there's definitely Irish in your background, and an ancestor who kissed the blarney stone."

"Sorry, you're wrong. But we Frenchmen can be pretty damned charming, too. Remember *Frenchman's Creek*." He was growing serious again, facing her with an expression that made her heart race.

Yes, Andrew Drack, you definitely have charm...far too much for a woman to stay with you among these dancing shadows, brandy warming her innards, and still be able to resist.

"Sorry, I'm making you ill at ease." He settled back on the couch. "Relax. This blind guy is backing off. Tell me about yourself, your family. If we're going to be friends, we should know a little about each other." He smiled.

Struggling to bring herself back to a cool reality, she hesitated.

"Come on." He encouraged with an all-out grin. "Let's have it. I'm pretty sure a successful photographer doesn't come from a long line of serial killers or gangsters."

"Not much to tell." She shrugged. "I'm a freelance photographer from Ottawa. My parents are retired schoolteachers. Presently they're traveling in Europe. My only sibling is a brother. He's ten years my senior and a commercial airline pilot. The last time I heard, he was on the London-to-Cairo run."

She told the truth about her family to lessen the lies she had to keep straight. She couldn't see how it would matter, given in such general terms.

"Real jet setters." A note of contemplation slid into his tone. She didn't like it, not one bit. Small spiders of suspicion started to chase one another up and down her spine.

"Not really. Mom and Dad saved for this trip for years. Barry travels in his work."

"What about you? Have you ever been to Europe?"

"Hardly," she scoffed. "Do you know what an...a freelance photographer makes?" *Oops. Nearly made a slip there.*

"Approximately."

"Well, then, good. Does that mean this inquisition

is at an end?"

"Is that what it sounded like?" He raised an eyebrow. "If we hadn't banished a certain five-letter word from the vocabulary of Phantom Island, I'd use it now. Instead, I'll simply say it's your turn."

"Okay. Tell me all about Andrew Drack."

"My mother is a doctor, my father a lawyer in Vancouver," he replied. "I have two sisters, one happily married and mother of three totally obnoxious, totally lovable little boys; the other, a chartered accountant and dyed-in-the-wool career woman."

"What about you? What does Andrew Drack do when he's not living on a deserted island?"

"Something he won't ever do again." He hunched forward, his hands clasped between his spread knees.

"Why not? All workplaces these days are constructed to facilitate handicapped people. There's no reason that after a period of adjustment…."

"Damn it, yes, there is." He jumped to his feet and went to stand in front of the fireplace. "I was a photographer."

"Andrew…" Danielle couldn't find an adequate reply.

Oh, God, what could be worse? The man was a professional, perfectly capable of seeing through her fake livelihood.

"Stuck for words?" He swung back to her, his face working with emotion. "I know I was when they told me my career was over." He strode to the closet in the foyer and pulled it open to reveal the jumble of valises. "You wanted to know about my life? Well, there it is. A pile of junk in a closet."

"Andrew…" His name kept repeating like a

hiccup, but she couldn't seem to stop it. She joined him by the open door.

"No longer a photographer, no longer even a man who can have lighted candles ready when he invites a woman to dinner," he muttered. His fingers searched among the fabrics of the garments in the closet until her found her jacket. He took it from its hanger above the equipment and handed it to her. "You'd better go. Aladdin and I will walk you home. I'm sure you've had enough of this romantic evening." Sarcasm colored the last two words.

"You don't have a very high opinion of women if you think they can be put off by a small handicap, if you think..."

She didn't get a chance to finish. She was in his arms and he was kissing her, kissing her deeply. His body full length against hers was hard though the soft shirt and casual pants. As his mouth moved over hers with thoroughly arousing expertise, Danielle realized with what was left of her sanity that he'd had lots of practice. She didn't care.

Finally, when she believed she was floating, borne on the wings of his incredible sensuousness toward a place of pure erotic pleasure, he drew away and ran the backs of the fingers of his left hand down her cheek. Her breath somersaulted in her throat.

"This is where I should invite you to stay the night," he said softly and kissed her parted lips again, lightly this time, but with the desire to linger as clear as glass. "But I can't. Firstly, you're confusing the daylights out of me right now, and secondly, my self-confidence needs more recovery time. At this point, I'm not sure I wouldn't simply embarrass myself."

"Just as well." She struggled to make her words sound cool and controlled as she fought to bring her raging physical needs under control. "I'm not ready for that much commitment…yet."

"Commitment?" He drew back and faced down at her. "Is that what spending the night with me would mean to you? A commitment?"

She nodded.

"I guess you're not into one-night stands."

"Did you think I might be?" She looked up at him, surprised.

"In my former profession I met a lot of female photographers and photojournalists. A fair number of them thought nothing of jumping into bed with a man for a night and leaving before breakfast. I'm glad you're different, Dani Breckenreid. Now I'm going to take you home before my confidence returns full force."

****

They headed up the moonlit beach toward the cottage, Aladdin in his harness leading Andrew. A cold calm lay over land and water. The clouds had retreated and moonlight cast soft, mysterious shadows over the sand. Snuggling down in Hester Matthew's jacket, Danielle believed frost would cover the island before morning.

"It's three years ago this month since the Fire Ship put in its last reported appearance," she said, glancing out over the glassy bay. "One of the old newspaper articles I found among the books in the cottage gave a report of it. There were quite a number of such stories, dating back over the past hundred years or so. Miss Matthews must have collected tales of the sightings.

According to these past experiences, it's due to show up again soon...if it ever does. Did you know some scientists believe it's merely a collection of gases from submarine coal beds breaking through the water under specific conditions? Others declare it's a mutant form of St. Elmo's fire. Then there's the theory that it's a combination of escaping gases and changing currents."

"That's pretty mundane stuff. I don't know much about the Fire Ship, but I thought there was a lot more romance and adventure connected with it."

"Oh, you mean the legends." She paused and looked up at him. "I discovered lots of those. Would you care to hear a few?"

"Definitely."

"The atmosphere is perfect for telling ghost stories. Let me settle you in an appropriate location to enjoy them. There's a driftwood log behind you."

"Ah, ghost stories on a dark, lonely beach." He eased himself down onto the log. "Sit, Aladdin. Dani is about to try to scare the beejeebers out of us."

"Of course not!" she protested, then, catching his teasing mood, continued more slowly, "but it *is* a tempting idea."

"Get to the story, woman. My teeth can't wait to start chattering."

"Okay, okay." She sat down beside him.

"Closer." He held out his arm. "I may need serious comforting."

"Wimp," she taunted. "I've already told you I can recognize a come-on."

"Can't blame me for trying. If you're not ready to be seduced, get on with the story."

"The earliest stories declare the Fire Ship to be the

ghost of a sixteenth-century Portuguese vessel whose captain betrayed one of the local Indian tribes," she began. "In retribution, they boarded his ship one night, as it lay at anchor off this coast, and captured the traitor and his crew."

"Another pirate story." Andrew shrugged one shoulder. "You'll have to do better than that."

"Okay. Try this for a knee-knocker. The Indians decided on an especially insidious death for the captain." Danielle's voice grew low and cryptic. "They tied him to a large rock just off shore at low tide and listened to him begging for mercy as he was slowly drowned by the incoming water."

"Interesting but hardly hair raising." Andrew shrugged his other shoulder. "So where does this fire thing come in?"

"The next summer, when the captain's brother came searching for him, he found his ship still riding at anchor, a deserted ghost. He and his crew boarded the vessel only to find a band of First Nations men lying in ambush.

"The Portuguese sailors, seeing the hopelessness of their position, decided to fight to the death. Determined not to die without taking as many of their attackers as possible with them, they set the ship on fire. Supposedly it's the ghosts of those desperate sailors whom people claim to have seen scrambling up the rigging of the Fire Ship in a vain attempt to avoid the flames. Legend has it only one First Nations man involved in the bloodshed managed to escape and swim to shore. That's how the story survived."

"Where's the romance, the damsel in distress, et cetera?"

"Okay, try this one." Danielle settled more comfortably beside him. "A young bride was abducted and ravaged by pirates, who later sailed their vessel into this area. Here, retribution caught up with them. The picaroons found their ship mysteriously engulfed in flames. Legend declares their souls were forever doomed to sail here at the mouth of Chaleur Bay aboard the flaming vessel. Does that meet your criteria for a romantic tale?"

"Too sad. Definitely too sad. And not nearly romantic enough. Especially on a night like this."

She looked over at him. His face hidden by the glasses and shadows told her nothing, but his voice—half-teasing, half-suggestive—made her feel like a teenager with her first crush.

Then out of the tail of her eye she saw it.

"Andrew! The Fire Ship!"

Chapter Seven

"What…?" he began, but she was scrambling away from him and bouncing to her feet.

"The Fire Ship! Out there on the bay! I have to get my camera! Wait here. I'll be right back!"

"Dani…"

Ignoring him, she raced off up the beach toward the cottage and jammed the key into the lock, all but bending it. Inside she snapped on a light, grabbed her new camera and tripod, and raced back to the beach. In her haste, she left the door ajar.

"Hold the tripod steady while I settle the camera!" She thrust the three-legged stand into his hands.

"Does it look like three orange gas jets shooting out of the bay?" Running his hands over the apparatus, he spread the tripod's legs and faced out over the water.

"Yes!" Danielle stopped screwing the camera into place and stared at his profile. "Andrew, can you see it?" She grasped his arm.

"I told you I can distinguish night and day." He didn't shift his gaze from the burning ship. "Don't delude yourself. It's not a miracle. Now get to work." He turned to her. "There's no way of knowing how long that thing will remain visible."

"Right." She put her eye to the viewfinder and focused on the image that looked like a three-masted ship in flames. Hands trembling, she eased the zoom in until she thought she could actually see sailors clambering up the fiery masts.

Trembling with excitement, she estimated the length of exposure for a night shot, using the method she'd found described in those old photography books. Her heart racing, she depressed the shutter. A second later her hands fell to her sides and she groaned.

"What is it? It's still there! Get snapping!"

"The camera's lost its charge." She sank down and covered her face with her hands.

Andrew, seated on the sand, put his hands behind his neck, lowered his head between his knees, and emitted a groan.

"Oh, no!" She stared as the ship vanished into the night. "It's gone."

"How can that camera not be charged?" Andrew raised his head. "You just bought it this morning."

"It was charged when we left the store. I must have somehow left it turned on and the power drained."

Oh, God, how lame that sounds…and yet it's the truth. Stupid, stupid, stupid. No professional photographer would have done something like that.

"Ah, hell!" His words were a moan.

She swallowed hard. She hadn't expected to share the island with a former professional photographer. Her cover had seemed safe. Now, fear of exposure coiled around her heart.

"Stop being so condescending!" Desperate for a response that would throw him off the trail, she flew back at him. "How do I know *you* aren't in league with the ghost? How do I know *you're* not working some crazy scheme to scare me off the island and get your privacy back?"

"Right!" He grasped Aladdin's harness and pulled himself to his feet. "A lot of my buddies are ghosts! Why don't you just come clean? A real photographer wouldn't have missed two mind-blowing photos in the space of two days. Who are you, Dani Breckenreid? What's the real reason you came to Phantom Island?"

He towered over her. Galvanized, she stared up at him. The air between them seemed to crackle with the intensity of their emotions. Every fiber in her body seethed; his passion, even in anger, enthralled her, mesmerized her beyond anything she could have imagined.

"I think I'll have Wade run your fingerprints through the RCMP computer," he said turning back in the direction of his farmhouse. His tone was suddenly cold, calculating. "You left some good ones, I've no doubt, on the wine glass and the brandy snifter. The results could be interesting."

"No!" Danielle leaped to her feet and grabbed him by the arm.

Aladdin snarled a warning, and she jumped back.

"It seems we've hit a nerve." He rounded back to face her. "Maybe you'd rather level with me. Maybe that way we can keep Wade out of it."

She hesitated. No way did she want the fingerprints she'd so conveniently left about his house run through a police computer. She had no doubt that by now that computer would have her fingerprints on file from the museum—along with her identity as the suspected perpetrator of the Egyptian heist.

"Okay, okay!" she snapped and believed she knew how an animal trapped in a cage felt. "I'll tell you."

"My place or yours?" he asked, so coldly calm an

icy chill washed over her.

****

"I *am* a photographer," she began a few minutes later as they sat in her living room. "Just not a good one."

Andrew had taken a chair across from her, his decision distancing her from him emotionally as well as physically. She paused and dug deep inside to become a convincing actor playing the role of Dani Breckenreid.

"Really?" The word reeked of a piercing skepticism that slashed at her self confidence.

"Yes, really." She drew a deep breath and hurried along. "I had a job with an Ottawa newspaper…a rookie, actually, low man on the assignment priority list because of my inexperience."

"Had? You don't work there anymore?" His questions had begun to sound like an all-out interrogation.

"No." She shook her head and looked down at her hands clasped in her lap. "I muffed my first major assignment. Just like tonight, I forgot to check my camera when I was sent to take a photo of a meeting between the U. S. President and our Prime Minister. It jammed, and I'd forgotten my backup in the car." Getting into the spirit of her role, she stood and began to pace. "I only got the assignment because there was a flu epidemic and all the other photographers were sick. It was my big chance to prove myself, and I blew it…totally, completely."

Her voice rose, then fell, and she sank back onto the couch to cover her face with her hands. After a few seconds of silence, she peeked though her fingers to see if Andrew was buying her story. Even though she knew he couldn't see her, acting out the part helped her with the words.

He had leaned forward in his chair, resting his elbows on his spread knees, rubbing his palms together in a slow, thoughtful gesture.

"So you came here to lick your wounds, is that what I'm supposed to believe?" he asked.

"No!" She dropped her hands and took up her story. "I came here to get an absolutely unique shot, one that would establish me once and for all as a really competent professional photographer. Can you imagine the sensation a photo of the Fire Ship would cause? Offers would roll in. *National Geographic* would be at my door... But most of all, my editor would be *so* very sorry she fired me and didn't have exclusive rights to my work. Now I've flubbed that possibility with flying colors...twice."

Her voice, which had been rising again, dropped with disappointment.

"So that's it? That's your story? All of it?"

She looked up at him and saw his lips drawn into a hard, unrelenting line. He didn't believe her! Panic raced through her veins.

"That's it." She struggled for flippant. "Take it or leave it."

"Come on, Aladdin." He got to his feet. "It's time we headed for home. I have a lot of thinking to do."

The dog got up from where he'd been dozing by the hearth, stretched, and moved to brush against his master's leg. Andrew caught the handle of the harness in his hand.

"Forward," he instructed the dog, and together they headed for the door. There he paused. "This thing between us has been moving way too fast for a blind guy to handle." He spoke with his back to her. "I can't decide if what you're telling me is the truth or one gigantic fabrication from start to finish. I've never found liars particularly attractive, Dani, so until I sort things out in my head, let's just cool it."

"Fine by me." The words, sounding casual and natural, hurt at the back of her throat. "Good night, Andrew."

****

Andrew Drack walked back to his house trying to come to some conclusion about Dani Breckenreid. The evening, instead of clarifying his impression of her, had only left him more confused.

What he found most troubling was her apparent sweet innocence. Her kiss had at first been as light as the brush of a butterfly's wing, then as soft as a dewy morning, and finally all-out passionate and sensuous, with an exploratory freshness about it that had almost brought him to the breaking point. She might not be sixteen, but she had all the nubile innocence of a hopeless romantic waiting for the guy on the white horse. Her remarks regarding one-night stands had made that clear.

He made a disgruntled sound deep in his throat. Aladdin stopped and looked up at him.

"It's okay, boy," he reassured the dog. "I'm thinking about heroes on horses. Let's go home. I'm cold and tired, and I need to think."

As they once more started toward the crumbling farmhouse, he wondered how Wade's evening had turned out. It had to have been better than his.

Chapter Eight

Once again his voice awakened her.

She came to consciousness in the corner of the living room couch where she'd finally fallen asleep, the old afghan wrapped around her. Sitting up, she yelped. A sharp kink in her neck took her by surprise, and it hurt. Staggering to her feet, she grabbed up the flimsy robe that matched her equally flimsy nightgown, two pieces of the collection she'd packed for that romantic weekend in Montreal, and headed for the door. Pulling it open, she faced him.

"What?" She pushed tangled hair back from her face, so drowsy it wasn't until a cold draft of ocean breeze hit that she realized what she was wearing. Reflexively she wrapped her arms around her body.

"Good morning," he greeted her as if nothing was amiss. *What would he think if he could see me in this get-up? Definitely not deserted-island-ghost-hunting gear. But he can't, right?*

"You must have absolutely no shame!" Secure in the fact, she faced him angrily. "I'm amazed you have the temerity to show your face around here after last night!"

"I said I needed some time on the romance level, that's all," he replied. "There's no reason we can't be friends, is there?"

"Oh, but I think there is." She strode into the

113

kitchen, where she pulled a coffee can from the cupboard and slammed it down on the counter. "After you suggested I was lying to you, after you decided to downgrade that 'something more than friendship'? Oh, come on!"

She started to swing away, but she discovered he'd followed her. As her shoulder bumped his chest, he grabbed her in his arms and suddenly he was kissing her, kissing her with a strength-sapping, resolve-melting power far beyond that which had turned her knees to jelly the previous evening; this transformed her innards to a ball of crackling flame.

"Good God, what are you wearing?" When he finally released her lips, he ran his hands down her body and sucked in a sudden breath.

"A negligee… None of your business!" She jerked free and backed off. "If you'll excuse me, I'll put on something more appropriate for a rational discussion."

"No need on my account." A corner of his mouth quirked up.

"Well, there is on mine. But I'll start the coffee before I get dressed."

****

"Dani, I want to believe you." He was sitting at the table ten minutes later when she returned dressed in what was fast becoming her ubiquitous uniform of jeans and sweatshirt. "But your stories just don't hang together. I had to tell Wade about your horseman sighting, just in case—"

"Why on earth would you tell Constable James?" Astounded, Danielle stared at him incredulously. "After you joked about the sighting, after you said the horseman was a figment of my overactive imagination?"

"I had a reason."

"What reason? Did you find my story so amusing you thought you'd give your Mountie friend a good belly laugh with it?" The coffee had finished dripping into the pot, and she headed for the refrigerator.

"Try life or death."

"What?" She stopped abruptly in taking out a container of coffee creamer. "Whose life? Whose death?"

"Mine. Hadn't you better close that door? I feel a draft. Your food will spoil."

"How could telling Constable James about my horseman sighting possibly be of life and death significance to you?" She placed the carton on the table and let the refrigerator door click shut behind her.

"Listen and learn."

"Okay, okay. Just get on with your story…whatever it is." She plunked two slices of bread into the toaster.

"First you'd better sit down. What I'm about to tell you might just knock you off your feet." His tone became ominously serious.

"Okay. Sitting." She took the chair opposite him. *Good God, what's he about to say?*

"I'm in the witness protection program. I told Wade about the horseman because I thought that guy on the horse might be someone sent to kill me."

"Good God! What did you…witness?" The toast popped, and she flinched.

"I can't tell you. Actually, I did much more than witness. I inadvertently took a photo of a major crime in progress. The perpetrators saw me and lit out after me. In the ensuing car chase, my jeep blew a tire and rolled into a ditch. My camera equipment was ruined, but before those guys could get to me and discover that fact, a police cruiser arrived, so I was later told. I was unconscious at the time.

"When I came to in the hospital, the Mounties asked what had happened. When I told them, they were elated. I had become an eyewitness who could put away a couple of major crime figures they'd been after for years."

"But you'd been blinded, your cameras destroyed." Numbed by his revelations, Danielle struggled to digest the heavy meal of information, but it clogged her mind, made her dizzy with a sense of unreality.

"Yes, but *they* didn't know that. The RCMP asked if I'd go along with a plan to worry those guys, maybe lure them into a mistake by keeping the destruction of my camera and eyesight a secret. When I agreed, they sent me into hiding here, under Wade's protection."

"And I'm supposed to believe all that? It sounds like the plot of a badly written thriller."

"It's the best I can do." He shrugged.

"Exactly where did this witnessing, high speed chase, et cetera, occur? Can you provide that information to give at least a ring of truth to your story?"

"On the British Columbia coast," he said. "Not far from my parents' summer home. That's another reason they sent me here. It's as far away from the scene of the crime and my family as possible and yet still within RCMP jurisdiction and protection."

"With only Constable James as your guardian?" She had to fight not to believe him, to throw up barriers against it. It all made a weird kind of sense.

"Bringing in a battalion would arouse suspicion, don't you think?" That irresistible grin began at the corners of his mouth. "I'm confident Wade can handle the job. He's one of the best. I have known him since University." He shifted in his chair. "And Jimmy Waters monitors all comings and goings on the island. Although he's not aware of the facts as I've told you, he does know I'm in some kind of trouble and that Wade is guarding me. And don't forget Aladdin. Now, please, can we leave my past alone and get on with being friends? I've trusted you with my life, so I think I can safely presume that much in our relationship."

She hesitated. "How do I know you're telling the truth?"

"You don't." He shrugged again. "This time I can't call Wade to confirm my story. He'd be a whole lot less than happy if he found out I'd confided in you. So I guess here's where you have to decide if you can trust me."

"Have you decided to believe I'm a not-too-competent photographer?"

He hesitated. "Fair enough. Fine, I'll believe you."

"Okay, so we're even...sort of." She stood and headed for the toaster. "Jam or peanut butter?"

"Jam."

****

She placed a slice of buttered toast and a glass of orange juice against his fingers on the table and sat down opposite him with hers. "I take it this decision to confide in me hit you like an epiphany. Otherwise you wouldn't have felt the need to come over here at seven a.m."

"Seven a.m.? Hey, you are sleepy. It's eight o'clock. What's wrong? Didn't you sleep well?

"Not really."

He paused before he continued slowly and carefully, "Would you like Aladdin and me to move in for a few days? Your couch is decently comfortable, and lately we've been finding the nights pretty lonely at the farmhouse."

"Thank you, but I'll be fine. I'm planning to go on the offensive and find out where this spook hides his horse."

"I don't think that's a good idea." He paused abruptly with the juice glass halfway to his mouth. "If he's in league with those guys who are out to silence me, he's dangerous, not just to me but to anyone who gets in his way."

"You really think that's the case?"

"It makes sense." He lifted a shoulder. "Since I'm assuming you don't have anyone pursuing you, I'm the logical target for any unexplained presence on Phantom Island, right?"

The question hung in the air.

"Right?" he repeated.

"Oh, yes, right, of course."

"So now you understand why I don't think your going looking for the horseman's mount is a good idea."

When she was once again slow to reply, he pressed, "Don't you?"

"Listen, Andrew." She faced him, deadly serious. "All my life I've done the safe thing, the sensible thing. None of that careful living has paid off. It certainly didn't prevent my losing my job and ending up here on a ghost-infested island. Maybe all this is some sort of sign, a sign that it's time for me to get out there and start taking a few risks. If the horseman does prove to be someone out to get you, maybe I can do something to stop him."

"Dani…"

"I promise to be careful, Andrew. If I do unearth anything even remotely dangerous, I'll report back to you, and you can decide the next step. Agreed?"

He turned away from her. "Dani…"

"Agreed?" This time it was Danielle who repeated the question, and she did it in a tone that brooked no refusal.

"Okay, but don't take any crazy risks."

"Don't worry. I'm no hero."

"Good. I like you the way you are."

"Thank you." She stood and began to gather up the dishes.

"Appearances to the contrary, I didn't come here to bum another breakfast or to tell the story of my misfortunes." He hesitated, and Dani could sense his uneasiness. "I've been trying to ease into asking a favor. But if you've got plans to start a major sleuthing operation…"

"Favor?"

"I need a drive into New Harbor for a doctor's appointment," he said. "Wade tried to arrange his schedule so he could take me, but his plans fell through at the last minute."

She caught the embarrassment in his tone and in the way he dropped his head as if he were looking at his hands.

Damn, what can I do? The man needs a drive. To a

doctor. It shouldn't be any more risky than when we went to buy that camera equipment.

"Okay," she said. "I can look for the horseman later. Unfortunately, I'm sure he'll still be around. What time do you have to be in town?"

"Two o'clock. I'll call Wade to alert Jimmy to come and get us."

****

As he walked back up the beach toward his house a few minutes later, he felt torn, indecisive, and, worst of all, ineffectual. He shouldn't have kissed her. It had been a knee-jerk reaction. He hadn't given in to one of those in years. He couldn't afford to start now.

Forgetting how good she'd felt in his arms in that sexy nightgown—the way her body had fit so neatly into his, the way his senses had reacted, as if he were a seventeen-year-old on his first hot date—wouldn't be easy, either. And he couldn't forget her plan to seek out the horseman in an effort to keep him safe. If she was faking concern, she was doing one hell of a job of it.

Cool it. This is just another job. Once I connect the dots between her and Hank Rockenfeller, it'll be over, and I'll be free to move on to other things. Dani Breckenreid will be just a memory...a very sweet, very hot, very tantalizing memory.

Chapter Nine

At one o'clock they disembarked from Jimmy Water's decrepit ferry in her pre-owned vehicle. Aladdin was stretched out full length across the back seat.

"Stop a minute, if you don't mind," Andrew surprised her by requesting. "I'd like a word with Jimmy."

"Do you need help?" she asked as he opened the door and started to get out.

"No, I'll be fine." He found the rear door handle and let Aladdin out to act as his guide.

Danielle watched as he made his way back to the barge and fell into what appeared to be a serious conversation with the old man. Jimmy Waters talked animatedly, frequently waving an arm out toward the bay and Phantom Island. Her curiosity about their conversation was thoroughly piqued by the time both men turned back toward her car.

When they arrived, Jimmy opened both doors on the passenger side for Andrew and Aladdin. When he hobbled around to Danielle's door, she wound down her window, assuming he wanted to speak to her.

"How's things out there?" he asked. "Makin' out okay, are ya?"

"Fine, Jimmy, thanks to your preparations. I wish you'd let me compensate you."

"Ah!" He waved aside the idea with a gnarled hand. "Hettie and me... We was real good buddies. Takin' care of her place and them what lives in it is the best I can do ta honor her memory."

"Did everyone call her Hettie?" Danielle asked remembering how Harry had referred to her as "Aunt Hester."

"Well, her proper name was Hester, a'course, but anyone what knew her a'tall called her Hettie."

"I think we should be on our way," Andrew interrupted. "Getting close to my appointment time."

"Then, git." Jimmy moved back from the car to give them clearance. "I'll be here ta take ya back at five o'clock sharp. This thing ain't safe ta have out on the water after dark. Might scare off that ghost out there on your island, it's so pretty!" He squeaked out a chuckle and turned back to his ragtag craft.

"That's good old Jimmy." Andrew chuckled. "Completely reliable, heart of gold, and sharp as a tack."

Danielle glanced over at her passenger before returning her attention to her driving. Was there something going on between the old man and Andrew Drack? Had they perhaps teamed up to get someone to play ghost on the island and scare her away?

Don't be fanciful, Danielle Burgess. Next you'll think Bibsy is some kind of spy disguised as a cat.

When they arrived in town, Danielle let Andrew and Aladdin out at the medical clinic. After his assurance that they'd be fine without her, she drove to the small town's only shopping mall. She planned to spend the time purchasing groceries and other items. Glancing at a public phone booth she passed on the way, she thought of trying to contact Harry.

No, no, no. So far no one has found me. Contacting him could ruin all that.

****

An hour and a half later, when she returned to the medical center to pick up Andrew, she found him waiting for her at the curb. It had begun to rain, but he seemed oblivious to the fact, his face grim, his right hand clamped to the handle of Aladdin's harness.

"Hi!" She leaned across the seat to open the passenger door. "Ready to head home?"

He grunted something she took to be an affirmative as he let Aladdin precede him into the car and waited for him to leap over the seat into the rear. Deciding to give him time to come to terms with whatever was troubling him, Danielle turned up the speed of her wipers as the rain increased, and she pulled out onto the road without further comment.

"Would you like a coffee or a soft drink?" She saw a roadside convenience store ahead.

"No." His expression hard and grim, he faced straight ahead. "All I want is to live my life the way I choose. Today I learned that's not going to be possible."

"Andrew…"

"Don't say you're sorry, Dani. At this moment in my life, you can't be half as sorry as I am." He was angry now, angrier than she'd ever seen him.

"Actually, I was going to say it didn't matter…to me." She snapped on her signal light and turned off the highway onto the pot-holed secondary road to Cavalier's Cove. "Not the fact that you're hiding out, that you've been injured…"

"Pull over," he said. "We have to talk."

"Okay." She did as he instructed, shoved the gearshift into Park, and turned to face him, her back against the driver's door. "Talk."

"I have to stop seeing you…spending time with you, that is." He leaned back in the seat with a weary sigh. "I should have known better right from the start."

"Andrew, I don't understand. What did the doctor say? Or"—her words slowed—"do you have someone else? Someone from before your accident?"

"Not another woman, no." He turned away to face his side window. "Dani, I'm not the man for you. That was pointed out to me today in all its harsh realities. I should have realized it, should have accepted the fact before things went this far."

"If it's because you're blind, I don't care." She put her hand on his arm, but he shrugged her off.

"Accept the fact that our relationship is over. It's best for both of us." The old bitterness, this time harsh and biting, snapped from his words.

"But, Andrew…"

"No buts about it. Let's head back to the island. Jimmy will be waiting for us." He turned to face out the passenger window.

Stunned, she didn't move to comply. The windshield wipers swished back and forth, and the motor of the old car coughed.

"Okay." Coming back to the moment, she drew a deep breath and, turning to face forward, eased the vehicle into drive. She could see further argument was pointless.

For a few minutes they drove in silence, only the purr of the motor and the swish of the windshield wipers penetrating the interior of the vehicle.

"Your parents," he surprised her by saying suddenly. There was a new tenor in his voice, one that sent a shiver tingling up her spine. "Do they travel in Europe often?"

"I told you, this is their first time." The reply snapped out. "They saved for years to be able to go, but it's really none of your business...anymore."

She blinked back the tears threatening to spill down her cheeks.

"Why would they have to save? You told me your brother's a commercial pilot. Wouldn't they get special consideration to fly wherever they chose as often as they chose?"

"Of course, but my brother couldn't fly them around continental Europe and the British Isles. Touring those regions for two months takes money. They're not exactly backpacking, you know. I think this is the point where I'd ask to have my attorney present if you were a police officer," she said, the thought startling her as it flashed into her mind. "Since you're not, I'll simply refuse to answer."

"On the grounds it may serve to incriminate you?" he challenged. Again that new, unnerving tone. *What is happening here?*

"Incriminate me?" Danielle's heart was racing at triple speed, racing with the slashing bump of the windshield wipers battling the increasing downpour. "What *are* you talking about?"

"Forget it," he muttered. "Just forget it."

"Great!"

****

She was relieved when they finally entered

Cavalier's Cove. Clicking on her signal light, she turned into the lane leading to the ferry slip. "As soon as we're back on the island, I'll drop you off at your moldering manor. After that, I don't ever want to see you again."

"Suits me right down to the ground."

****

Twenty minutes later, he stood with Aladdin on the back step of his house as her tail lights vanished into the rain and mist.

Damn it. She's as clever as she is beautiful. One thing's for certain. This is one time I'm not going to enjoy going in for the kill.

****

Danielle unlocked the cottage door, shoved it open, and entered. She dropped her purse and her purchases onto the kitchen table before returning to slam it shut. Closing her eyes, she leaned back against the panel and tried to come to terms with what had happened. She and Andrew had ended their relationship.

What relationship? We're only two people who've ended up on this bleak bit of land in the middle of nowhere and had no one else to talk to, to share anything with. I'm being ridiculous. Simply because the man has some crazy sort of dark magnetism about him and sends me into a tailspin with his kisses...

A soft meow brought her out of her confused reflections. Looking down, she saw Bibsy twining herself around her ankles, staring up at her with round, bright eyes.

"Bibsy." She stooped and picked up the cat. The little animal purred and snuggled against her as she carried her into the living room and sank down on the couch.

"I've still got you, haven't I?" Danielle snuggled the small feline to her cheek. "Don't you dare run away and leave me all alone. I really need a friend just now."

As if on cue, Bibsy wrenched free and darted across the darkening room.

"Oh, great, so you're jumping ship, too…" Her words ended in a scream as something swooped down from above the fireplace and across the room over her head. Bibsy leaped after it.

Bat! I've got a bat in the house!

She ducked down on the couch, grabbing a pillow to hold over her head. Did they really tangle themselves in hair? Were there any poisonous ones in New Brunswick? Thoughts garbled in her mind and she cowered, listening to Bibsy's efforts to capture the intruder.

Suddenly, there was only silence. Cautiously she eased the cushion from her head and peered about the shadowy room.

"Bibsy?"

A half-meow, half-growl answered. Getting cautiously to her feet, she crossed to the wall and snapped on the light.

In the middle of the room, standing over her prey, Bibsy held the proud pose of one of her jungle relatives.

"You got it, Bibsy!" Danielle advanced toward the small black-and-white predator. "You're my hero…or heroine. It must have gotten in last night when I left the door open to run back to the beach with my camera for a photo of the Fire Ship. Andrew warned me not to leave any place for them to get in…especially at night."

Bibsy looked up at her, arched her back, and

fluffed out to twice her size.

"Now we have to dispose of the body." Danielle headed for the hearth and the fireplace tool that resembled a small shovel standing beside it. Bibsy melted back to normal size but remained with her conquest.

As Danielle returned with the instrument, the cat made a move to pick the body up in her mouth.

"No, no!" Danielle swooped in to scoop it up. "I've heard bats, even if they aren't directly poisonous, can be carriers of any number of terrible diseases."

Carrying the small corpse on the shovel, Danielle took it outside and deposited it in a covered garbage can at the corner of the house. Shuddering and shivering in the early evening darkness and rain, she scuttled back inside. In the bathroom she scrubbed at her hands. Although she hadn't actually touched the creature, she couldn't resist the urge to wash away any traces of germs it might have carried.

"Well, Bibs," she addressed the cat as she returned to the living room. "You're a hero. What would you like for a treat? I think a can of salmon would be a fitting reward."

A disgruntled meow replied.

"Okay, okay, so I deprived you of your prey." She headed for the kitchen. "You'll have to live with it. After all, you aren't lord of the island...not yet."

As she began to crank open the can of fish, her thoughts reverted to the man who had jokingly declared himself the island's ruler...Andrew...Andrew who was gone from her life. The incident with the bat had momentarily wiped it from her mind. Now it came back with all its depressing accruals.

****

Danielle measured coffee into the old percolator, added water, and headed out onto the veranda to get a breath of fresh air while it brewed. Surprised she'd slept well after the trauma of the previous day with Andrew's declaration and the bat incident, she was further amazed to see Andrew and Aladdin walking up the beach toward the cottage in the bright sunshine.

What now? Can't he simply leave it alone? Doesn't he feel anything? Doesn't he know opening an old wound...

Hands on her hips, she waited as he came closer. When he'd reached the marsh grass at the foot of the veranda steps, she spoke.

"I certainly didn't expect to see you."

"You're out and about already." He glanced in the direction of her voice.

"If you've come to mooch breakfast again, sorry. After yesterday, the less I see of you the better."

"I understand your feelings. I was pretty rough on you yesterday. The doctor's news was discouraging, but I had no right to take my disappointment out on you. Will you accept a humble apology? That's the reason I came...not to mooch a meal."

She hesitated. He was facing up toward her, a corner of his mouth tilting upward in the beginnings of a persuasive grin. Resolve-meltingly handsome, charming to the core, someone she truly enjoyed sharing time with...

"Okay...I guess. Come up on the veranda and take a seat. It's a beautiful morning. We can eat out here. I think one of these rickety chairs should hold you." She indicated the pair at the far end of the structure, then drew in her lips in exasperation. *The man is blind, stupid. Hasn't that sunk in yet?* Careful to make enough noise so that he could find the location, she dragged one forward.

"Thanks." He made his way up the steps. With Aladdin guiding, he found his way to the chair. "It is a fine morning," he breathed as he settled into it. "But Wade just contacted me via the CB and said a big storm is brewing. The tail end of a hurricane that hasn't diminished as it was supposed to. Be prepared to batten down the hatches. That's the second reason for my visit."

"The calm before the storm?" She looked out over the deadly still water.

"Something like that."

"We had a bit of a storm here last night." She paused before going back inside. "A bat apparently found its way inside the cottage and emerged last evening, shortly after I returned home. Fortunately, Bibsy caught it."

"Bibsy caught it?" He swung in his chair to face toward where she stood by the door. "A bat? Has she had her shots? Those things can carry all kinds of diseases."

"Oh, God! I don't know...I never thought...I've never owned a cat. What should I do?" Appalled, Danielle stared down at him.

"*We* call Wade on the CB and get him to send Jimmy out here asap. We have to get her to the vet in New Harbor right away. Where did you put the bat's body? We'll have to take it along to have it tested."

****

A half hour later they were headed toward New

Harbor as near the top of the speed limit as Danielle's old car could manage. Bibsy, wrapped in a towel fastened with a safety pin, yowled periodically from her confinement in the back seat. Aladdin sat pressed against the door as far from her as possible.

"Well, if you hadn't put up such a fuss about getting into the car, you wouldn't have to be trussed up," Andrew said, turning toward the noise. "We'll buy you a cat carrier in New Harbor for the drive home."

"And is she agreeable?" Danielle relaxed enough in her tense concentration on driving to throw him a quick grin.

"Okay, okay. So I'm getting attached to the little devil...even if she was a bit of a lioness to get into the vehicle."

"Andrew, you do think she'll be okay?" Danielle couldn't repress the remark any longer.

"Most likely. She was Hettie Matthews' companion. I'm sure that old lady took good care of her and her shots are up to date. We'll soon find out. Dr. Randolph is the only vet in miles. If Hettie took the cat anywhere in the vicinity it would have been to him, and he'll have records."

"And you know this how?"

"He's Aladdin's vet."

"Oh."

The remainder of the drive was silent except for Bibsy's frequent protests. When they arrived in the town, Andrew pointed her down a street to her left.

Sick with fear, Danielle took the struggling, yowling little cat from the back seat and, with Andrew and Aladdin beside her, made her way into the veterinary clinic.

****

"What a relief!" Danielle headed the old car back onto the road to Cavalier's Cove an hour later, Bibsy contained in a spanking new cat carrier in the rear, a toy mouse keeping her mostly quiet. "Hester was a good pet parent. Bibsy had every immunization imaginable."

"Pet parent?" Andrew grinned over at her. "I thought you'd never owned a cat."

"I haven't, but that's what Dr. Randolph's assistants called me when I went to pay the bill."

"Oh. So I take it you've decided to become her permanent caregiver?"

"Not much else I can do." She shrugged, glancing back over her shoulder at the little cat contentedly hunkered down on the pillow in her cage, the mouse between her front paws. "What with the vet bill and the cost of food and accessories at the pet store, I've got a major investment in her."

"Right. A major investment. Nothing more."

"What?" She glanced over at him.

"Nothing, nothing."

****

Back on the island, she drove Andrew and Aladdin home.

"Thanks for coming with us to the vet," she said as he got out and opened the rear door for the dog.

"Not a problem. Watch out for that incoming storm. Wade says it's supposed to be powerful."

"I will." She hesitated, not sure what she expected or wanted.

"Fine. Goodbye." He turned and, with the dog leading, limped toward the house.

With a sinking feeling, she shifted into drive and

turned the car back into the lane. He'd been so cool, almost like a stranger. But how could he be, after the time they'd spent together? After those hot, breathtaking kisses?

Stop it. Just stop it. He's made it clear how he wants things to stay between us. The most caring thing he said when he got out of the car was to be ready for a storm tonight. Not a very romantic parting note.

At the cottage, she released Bibsy. The little feline darted off into the marsh grass. Danielle was confident she'd be back. Clever feline that she was, she knew where to find food a whole lot easier than chasing down a mouse.

****

Ten minutes later, as Danielle was making a sandwich, the thought struck her. Andrew had *pointed out* the direction of the vet's office. She'd been so upset about Bibsy, she hadn't taken note of the fact at the time.

Or maybe she'd imagined it. She poured coffee into a cup and carried it with the sandwich to the coffee table in the living room. With an exasperated sigh, she sank down on the couch. Was nothing about this place what it seemed to be?

Glancing toward the window, she saw ominous clouds darkening the sky. The storm Andrew had warned her about was moving in. She shrugged. So what. She'd curl up with one of those photography books and wait it out.

****

A yowling at the back door aroused her. Lost in her reading she hadn't noticed the time passing, but a storm-induced early twilight had begun to darken the room. She stood, stretched, and went to let a small, disgruntled cat inside.

"I knew you'd be back when you got hungry," she said as Bibsy walked regally past her, tail and head held high. "Okay, give me a minute."

She fed the cat, made herself a snack of cheese, crackers, and tea, and decided she might as well prepare for bed. The gloomy evening promised to be fit only for curling up with a good book.

In the bedroom, as she glanced disdainfully at the suitcase holding those impractical clothes, an idea occurred to her. She hadn't investigated the dresser drawers. Maybe Hettie had some practical nightwear.

Pulling open the top drawer, she found a collection of no-nonsense underwear and white cotton socks. No thongs or lacy bras for Hettie Matthews, and she could use those sports socks. In the next drawer she found several neatly folded sweatshirts. Shaking them out, she decided they'd do while she washed the only one she'd brought with her.

In the last drawer she discovered several pairs of neatly folded flannelette pajamas.

"Perfect." She pulled out a pale blue jacket and pants with frolicking kittens decorating them. "Just the thing for a stormy night."

Minutes later, as she settled into the bed to read, Bibsy jumped up beside her, sniffed her outfit, then snuggled tight against her side.

"Oh, Bibsy." She laid a hand on the small head burrowing into the flannelette. "You remember. I underestimated you. You miss her, don't you. I'm so sorry."

Bibsy's response was a long, mournful-sounding

feline moan.

****

Danielle woke to the sound of waves crashing on the beach. Wind rattled the windows and howled down the chimney.

She got out of bed, shoved her feet into her running shoes, and padded into the living room to look outside. In the darkness, she saw mountainous waves rising out of the water like dark monsters. Horrible in size and intensity, they rushed across the sand to engulf the veranda and surround the cottage.

A plaintive meow and the now-familiar sensation of something brushing against her legs made her stoop and pick up a shaking Bibsy.

"It's all right, kitty," she comforted the little cat. "I don't think the water will rise any higher." Then, "Oh, God!"

A huge wave that made the others look like ripples was sweeping toward shore. It gushed to land with such intensity the old cottage flinched when it struck the veranda. A burst of water blinded the window behind which Danielle stood.

She gave a strangled cry and staggered backwards. Her sneakers made a squishing sound.

Water's coming inside! Oh, my God!

Hands seized her shoulders and she screamed. Whirling, she faced the horseman. Dressed in his traditional garb except for the plumed hat, a leather bandana covering his hair, he stood behind her, eyes looking directly into hers through the black mask obscuring the upper portion of his face.

He swept her up in his arms so swiftly she dropped the cat. Bibsy yowled as she hit the floor.

"Let me go!" Coming back to mobility, Danielle tried to break free but was held in a relentless grip. He carried her through the house and out the back door to where a black silhouette indicated the presence of his horse. Standing pastern deep in water, the animal shifted restlessly as less violent waves, their force lessened after hitting the cottage, washed around him. The horseman threw her into the saddle and prepared to swing up behind her.

Rescuing me. He's rescuing me. The realization burst over Danielle's reeling mind. Then another.

"Bibsy!" she cried. "Don't leave Bibsy!"

With a disgruntled sound somewhere between a curse and a guffaw, he whirled and ran back into the flooding cottage. Beneath her, the horse steamed and moved restlessly. She clung to the saddle and managed to stay in place as rain bucketed over both of them and the gale sent her hair slapping over her face in drenched clumps.

When he returned, he clutched a pillowslip that writhed and yowled above the blast of the storm's fury. Gathering up the reins, he vaulted up behind her, the fighting bundle in his hand.

As the storm raged and battled against them, he urged the horse to a fast trot through the water until they were on firm footing. Then, turning the animal, he headed down a trail into the forest at a smooth canter.

"Where are you taking me?" Danielle came sufficiently out of shock to yell above the roar of the wind.

Ignoring her, he kept the horse at a steady pace, all the time battling the screaming, roiling sack in his hand.

Finally, he drew rein and slid to the ground. He

pulled her down to join him and handed her the sack. Pointing ahead into the darkness to their right, he indicated a light glowing from a window. Through the deluge, she recognized their destination.

He'd taken her to the farmhouse on the safety of the cliff. Before she could speak, he remounted, swung the animal about, and vanished into the rain, wind, and darkness.

"Thank you," she yelled after him. She drew a deep breath, squared her shoulder, and headed for the light, fighting wind, rain, and the scrambling sack in her hand.

It took her some time to climb the path to the house, slipping and sliding up the rain-slicked incline. Buffeted by the storm, she staggered often. Several times she was nearly upset by the thrashing of the sack in her hand. After what seemed like an eternity, she stumbled onto the steps at the back of the house.

She pounded on the door. When she received no response, she tried the knob. The panel opened. She scuttled into the lighted kitchen, slammed the door on the inhospitable night, and placed her burden on the floor.

Bibsy clawed her way out of her pillowslip prison, shook herself, and paused to take in their new surroundings. Something that sounded like a growl issued from her throat.

"Don't be ungrateful, Bibsy." She pushed drenched hair back from her face and tried to come back to reality as she glanced around the dilapidated Victorian room. Surely this craziness wasn't happening. It all had to be a dream...a horseman-legend-induced dream. Being rescued by a ghost during a hurricane...a ghost willing to go back for a cat, rescued…in pajamas and running shoes.

Her present surroundings did little to bring reality to the situation. The room was a turn-of-the-century kitchen with cupboards of groove-and-tongue-board painted a sickly green, a chipped enamel sink with faucets mounted high on a rusted backboard, and a badly scratched wooden table and chairs. Cracked linoleum covered the floor, its floral design worn to a shadow. An ancient cooking stove sat in one corner. The only modern conveniences were a refrigerator, a microwave, and a coffeemaker.

A long, narrow window at the room's upper end was blotted by the clawing branches of a black spruce scratching viciously at the panes. The place smelled of mold and rotting wood.

Where is Andrew? Surely he's not out on such a night.

Another snarl from Bibsy made her turn toward the doorway leading to the hall. Framed in it stood Aladdin, hackles bristling. Beside him in plaid pajama pants, chest and feet bare, ubiquitous dark glasses in place, his hand clutching his cane, stood Andrew Drack.

"Is someone there?" he asked.

"Yes, Andrew. It's Dani. And Bibsy. Our cottage got flooded." She stopped short. How could she tell him she'd been rescued by a ghost?

"You walked all the way here? With the cat?" Incredulity colored his tone.

"Ran is more like it." Once into the lie, she had to keep it going. "We're both soaked."

"Of course. You'd have to be. I've a small fire going in the parlor. Can't trust a big one in this gale. Go in there and get warm while I find you something dry to put on. I assume you need it?"

"Yes." Her teeth chattered. "Please."

He turned back down the hall. Danielle started to follow, but Aladdin, yellow eyes bright with challenge, blocked the way. Bibsy, bristled as fully as her wet fur would allow, stood in mid-kitchen.

"Andrew, will you call off Aladdin? Bibsy needs to get warm and dry, too."

"Aladdin, come. Leave the cat alone."

With a final glare at the enlarged feline, the dog turned and followed his master down the hall and up the stairs.

Danielle and Bibsy dripped their way to the parlor to huddle in front of the fire. She wondered what Andrew Drack would have said if he could have seen her in drenched pajamas and running shoes that left a trail of wet splotches along the floor, never mind if he knew the actual manner in which she'd arrived at his house.

****

He came back, a navy terry robe in one hand, a large white towel in the other.

"Here." He handed them to her. "Get undressed. You can dry your clothes and shoes by the fire."

She hesitated.

"Oh, come on." The annoyed bitterness she'd heard come into his tone whenever his blindness became an issue returned. "You can't seriously be afraid I'll watch you undress."

"Andrew, I..." She stumbled over the words.

"Don't worry. Even if I could see, I wouldn't do anything like that. I like to think of myself as a kind of gentleman. Anyhow, you can rest easy. I'm going out to the kitchen to make us each a hot buttered rum."

Fool! she branded herself, and began to unbutton her pajama top.

By the time he'd returned with two mugs, she was wrapped in the robe, which hung to her ankles, had dried first her hair and then Bibsy's fur with the towel, put her clothing to dry by the fire, and was curled up on one end of the old sofa.

"Man, this is still one wild night." His good humor apparently restored, he held out a cup. She had to get up to take it. He was facing the wrong direction.

"It certainly is." She returned to her place in front of the fire. "I'm hoping I'll have a cottage to return to once it's over."

"I wouldn't worry. If it's as weatherbeaten and rugged as you've described, the old place has stood the ravishes of wind and water for a long time."

He started to sit down at the other end of the sofa. An indignant yowl stopped him halfway. Aladdin, who'd returned with him, snarled.

"Okay, okay, guys." Andrew straightened up and took a chair on the other side of the fire. "Cat, you've obviously claimed the couch for your mistress. Aladdin, Dani and her cat are guests in our home. Treat them as such."

With a mutter, the big dog lay down at his master's feet but continued to glare at Bibsy.

"Much better." Danielle heaved a sigh. "Thanks for bringing peace to the situation."

"Hopefully some day they'll learn to co-exist." He took a sip of his drink. "Now tell me what happened at the cottage and how you managed to get here in the wind and rain. It must be black as pitch out there."

"Yes, it is." Danielle looked at her pajamas and running shoes drying by the hearth. "I'm not really sure how I did it."

"You must have come up the shore. If you'd gone through the woods, you'd have gotten hopelessly lost."

"Of course." She took up the idea.

"But that wouldn't have been possible, with the tide so high and waves washing up as far as your cottage."

Oh, God, he's cornering me in a lie.

"I…that is…"

"Come on, Dani. The truth."

"I drove."

"Really? Through a flood? I didn't hear a vehicle. I've got excellent hearing. They say other senses get more acute after you lose one. With me it's the ability to detect sounds."

"Okay, okay. The horseman rescued Bibsy and me."

"The horseman? Damn it, Dani, you really are obsessed with this guy. How many times do I have to tell you he doesn't exist? Using him as a reason for your getting here is going way too far."

He paused, the mug clutched in both his hands. When he spoke again, his words shocked her.

"Are you a spy for those guys who are out to kill me?"

"What! Are you insane?" She banged her cup down on the table in front of her and leaped to her feet. "Good God, if I'd been sent by gangsters, I've had lots of opportunities to let them know where you are…or assassinate you myself!"

"Yeah, that makes sense." He appeared to calm down. "Okay, something miraculous happened and some wonderful being saved you and the cat. Let's leave it at that. I'm never going to get the truth out of you, and I give up trying. Drink your rum.

"I'll get you a pillow and blanket. Since I don't think any of the bedrooms aside from the one I'm using are habitable, you'll have to sleep on the couch with your watch cat. You'll be perfectly safe with that green-eyed monster on guard."

"No, let's *not* leave it at that." Courage returning, Danielle decided to confront him with the incident on the way to the vet that morning. "You *pointed* to the street where the vet's office was located. *Pointed*. What blind man can point out directions?"

"What?" Astonishment flashed from the word. "Pointed? You imagined it. Just like you've imagined the horseman. I couldn't point anyone in any direction, and you know it. You were upset about the cat. I simply told you to turn down Fishery Lane."

"No, no, no, you pointed!" She was on her feet, incensed.

"Dani, I'll get a couple of blankets. You need some rest. First you saw a blind man pointing out directions, and now you've been rescued by a ghost." He stood. "In the morning you'll see how ridiculous all this is." He crossed the room toward her and took the drink from her hands. "I don't think this is helping."

****

Danielle awoke to silence except for the drip, drip, drip of water. She moved and moaned. What was she sleeping on? A rock might be softer.

As full wakefulness caught up with her, she

remembered and struggled to a sitting position with a groan, the Victorian sofa creaking beneath her. Rubbing sleep from her eyes, she realized from the quietness that the storm must have blown itself out while she slept.

How could I manage to sleep through a hurricane in this gothic horror of a house with Count Dracula in residence?

She recalled the drink he'd given her. *That must have put me out like a light.* Her hand flew to her neck. *Definitely no vampire bites. Oh, come on, Danielle Burgess, get real. You don't honestly think...*

"Good morning." His voice made her start, and she looked up to see him coming into the room, two coffee mugs in his hands. He was dressed in jeans and a sweatshirt, definitely not vampire gear. "Did you sleep well?" He extended one of the cups toward the couch, but too high for her to reach.

"Too well." She clutched the robe about her and stood to take the steaming coffee. "What exactly did you put in that hot rum drink...besides rum? And how is it you're walking without Aladdin or your cane?"

"Here we go again." He heaved a sigh as he sank down on a chair. "Still don't trust me."

"Well?"

"Just rum. You were exhausted and disoriented from your run through the storm. Under those conditions, it probably hit you harder than normal. As for walking without assistance, this is my home. I know every bit of it by heart."

"Okay, if you say so." She looked at her pajamas and running shoes beside the now-dead fire. They appeared to be dry. She'd feel foolish walking home in them, but she had no choice.

"I have to be going." She took a quick sip of coffee, placed the mug on the table, and reached for her clothes. "I hope the water has receded enough for Bibsy and me to walk up the beach."

"I would guess it has." He went to a window and threw back the heavy drapes to let in a blast of sunshine. "I'm thinking it's a bright, clear morning. Would you like to have breakfast first? I owe you a couple. I'm pretty good at coffee and toast…here in my home."

"No, thanks just the same." She reached for her pajama top and the robe she was wearing fell open at the top. Hastily she clutched it back to her throat. "I'm sure the cottage will need a lot of cleaning after the storm, and…"

She paused and looked over at him.

"And what?"

"After what you said about not wanting to be involved with me, it's best I leave as soon as possible. Taking Bibsy to the vet was only a truce, as I see it."

There was a pause, and once again Danielle longed to be able to see his eyes, that she might gauge some measure of his emotions.

"Right. You're right." He swung about. "Where's the cat? Aladdin isn't growling. Hasn't run off, has she?"

"No." Danielle almost pointed to a bookcase in a corner. "She spent the night on a top shelf near the window. If you and the dog will leave us, I'll get dressed, coax her down, and we'll get out of your way."

"Sounds like a plan." He sucked in a deep breath. "Come on, Aladdin." Together they headed out of the parlor and down the hall toward the kitchen. "Goodbye,

Dani Breckenreid. It's been an experience."

Danielle found a lump in her throat so large she couldn't reply.

Chapter Ten

Hoping her activity level would help keep the cold at bay, Danielle jogged up the beach, shivering in her pajamas and running shoes. Although the sun shone and the ocean lay rippling with small, benign little waves, the October chill made it uncomfortable for anyone dressed as she was.

He hadn't accepted her tale of being rescued by the horseman, and she couldn't blame him. Ghosts don't exist, so how could she have been saved by one? She wished she hadn't told him, but the truth had seemed the only solution. Bad decision. All it had done was strengthen his resolve not to be involved with her.

But what difference does it really make? A relationship between us would never work out. He doesn't trust me. And anyhow, I have Harry...

Harry. She'd barely thought of him since she'd met Andrew. *Do I have Harry?* He'd made no serious commitment to her. On their aborted trip to Montreal, he'd promised to let her set the pace in their relationship right down to (he'd said) reserving separate rooms for them.

Since she'd met Andrew Drack, her hero worship for Harry Stone had faded. She hadn't realized it until Andrew had said he wanted no furtherance of their relationship. Only then did she realized Harry Stone had lost a good deal of his former appeal and a mystery man named Andrew Drack had taken his place.

But what did it matter now? She reached her cottage and made her way up steps strewn with seaweed and bits of driftwood. A major task awaited her in cleaning up the place while she awaited word the worse mess that was her life had been taken care of.

****

Danielle awoke the next morning to the sound of rain dripping from the eaves, feeling so miserable she thought she was catching something. Then she remembered. Andrew was gone from her life. With a prolonged moan, she rolled face down into her pillow.

This morning there'd be no handsome, affable man on her veranda. This morning there'd be no one to share breakfast, to banter with, to share the day. This morning would mark the first day of the rest of her life without Andrew Drack.

"Oh, God!" Dislodging Bibsy, who'd been curled up near the foot of her bed, she flopped over onto her back. The little cat yowled and tumbled up through the rumpled quilts to perch on her chest. Looking Danielle in the face, she yowled again, this time appealingly, eyes expectantly wide.

"Food. You want food, right? Well, good. Something to do instead of think. Very good."

She got up, shoved her feet into her running shoes, pulled on her robe, and shuffled into the living room, ruffling her tangled hair with her fingers. Was this the best she was going to feel this morning, every morning? She sincerely hoped not. Yesterday she'd been so involved with cleaning up the cottage after the storm she'd had little time to speculate about Andrew. Now...

Pushing aside the drapes, she saw the bay, dark and

rain-pocked, in a morning that looked miserably cold and desolate. Shivering, she went to build a fire on the hearth.

She wished she dared contact Dr. Harrison in Halifax but quickly squashed the idea. Even if she went to the mainland and used a pay phone, the police might be able to trace the call, might actually have a tap on the curator's phone on the chance the artifacts would be ransomed. Furthermore, she had no way of knowing if he was out of hospital yet or if, worst case scenario, he hadn't survived to be released. No, definitely, she shouldn't try to reach Dr. Harrison. Harry would come through as promised. He had to.

Fifteen minutes later, with a crackling blaze driving the chill from the cottage, she curled up on the couch, her breakfast of orange juice, toasted English muffin, and coffee on the low table in front of her. Bibsy came stealthily out of the bedroom, looked about, and stretched luxuriously before hopping up beside her, purring like a well-tuned motor.

"Now you get up," she said, rubbing the animal's velvety head. "Since you didn't come when I called you, you'll have to wait until I finish my breakfast to get some of that over-priced gourmet cat food I bought at the pet store. Here, have a bit of muffin and strawberry jam."

Bibsy examined the food skeptically before settling down to sample it.

"What will we do without them, Bibsy?" She stroked the little cat's head gently. "Don't pretend you won't miss Aladdin. He was as big a challenge to you as his master was to me. I have a feeling you enjoyed it."

She stood and went to stare out the window, her fingers wrapped tightly about her coffee cup. She needed its warmth. Why did he end it? What could have gone so terribly wrong while he was at the doctor's? Surely no medical doctor would tell him to end a relationship, especially when he didn't know the person involved. With an exasperated sigh, she returned to the coffee table to gather up her breakfast dishes.

Speculation was getting her nowhere. Worse than nowhere. She had to do something, and she knew exactly what that was. She had to start investigating Andrew Drack. That meant starting with the only clue available, the horseman. He was connected to Andrew, maybe not as a hit man sent to kill him, but in some way. As she headed into the bedroom to get dressed, she decided she'd start her investigation by finding the horse. It was the largest and most difficult of all the horseman's paraphernalia to conceal.

****

Twenty minutes later, dressed in jeans and sweatshirt, a pair of rubber boots she'd found on a boot tray near the back door (which fit decently enough when the toes were stuffed with socks), and a hooded rain jacket from a peg above them, she stood on the back doorstep and drew a deep breath of the clean, damp air. As she reached for the doorknob, Bibsy whipped past her. The little cat paused only a moment before darting off into the tangle of weeds and grass behind the cottage.

"Bibsy!" She held the door open. "Last call to get back inside before I leave."

She waited a few moments. When the cat didn't return, she closed the door and headed down the lane into the trees.

The rain had stopped, but the temperature was dropping. Her breath made fog in the cold air. Shivering, she struggled to ignore her discomfort and keep her thoughts focused on her mission. The phantom horseman needed a place to stable his mount; therefore, the barn behind Andrew's farmhouse would be the logical place to begin her search.

The overgrown trail through the trees was dark and shadowy and so silent the frost-encrusted fallen leaves crackling beneath her boots sounded abnormally loud.

A small gray animal scurried across in front of her. She jumped, gasped, then chided herself on her timidity and walked on. A mouse. Probably the island was full of them. That must have been how Bibsy had managed to survive during the months she'd been alone. She stuffed icy hands into her pockets and strode on with renewed determination.

When she reached the junction, she heard another rustling in the bushes. A disgruntled Bibsy emerged and yowled up at her.

"I appreciate your loyalty," she said. "But if you're going to be noisy and complaining, maybe you should go back to the cottage and wait for me under the porch. I gave you the chance to stay inside, remember."

Bibsy stared up at her with round, unblinking yellow eyes before sitting down in front of her.

"Okay, okay, you can come with me. But remember, silence is the word. Oh, look, Bibsy."

Almost hidden in the weeds was a heap of horse manure in the turning toward the farm.

"There is a real flesh-and-blood horse on this island," she breathed. "And it either came or went from

Andrew Drack's farm."

Trembling with anticipation, she moved stealthily down the trail until she could see the roof of the farmhouse through the branches. Off to the right, the corner of a dilapidated barn was visible above the scraggly conifers that surrounded the homestead.

She paused to examine the ground. No hoof prints, but the heavy rain in the night had probably wiped them out.

Hunched over to stay hidden by tall weeds and bushes, she scuttled toward a door at the side of the building. Her heart pounded, her entire body supercharged and ready for action.

The door stuck. She had to push hard before it yielded on rusted hinges with an eerie groan. She glanced toward the house. When nothing stirred, she eased her way inside. Something black dashed past her into the gloomy interior.

"Bibsy!" she hissed, expecting the silence to be shattered by whinnying and stamping when one devil-may-care feline startled a horse. To her relief, the only sounds were scurrying ones as Bibsy flushed something, probably a mouse.

When her eyes became accustomed to the gloom, she saw the barn was little more than a shell, gutted to become storage for the generator that provided power for the house, as well as an assortment of rusting farm equipment.

Danielle stifled her disappointment and eased her way back outside. Pausing, she glanced toward the house. It appeared deserted. If Andrew were there, Aladdin would have been raising an alarm by now.

It would be an excellent opportunity to learn more

about the man. If he happened to arrive while she was investigating, she'd say she'd come to borrow—she searched her mind—some electrical tape to fix her iron cord.

She strode across the center of the weed-choked yard to the house. If he was at home, she must appear to be arriving in a forthright manner. She went up the sagging steps and pounded on the weathered, windowless door.

"Andrew," she called.

Heart beating a mad tattoo, nerves tingling, Danielle eased open the door, flinched when it emitted a grating sound, and slid herself inside.

I'll check the cupboard drawers for electrical tape. That way if he happens to return, I'll have a valid reason for being here.

The first drawer held eating utensils, cheap tin implements dotted with rust spots; the second, a collection of faded, paper-thin dishcloths and towels.

She was opening the third when a slight sound made her whirl.

Andrew Drack and his wolf-dog stood framed in the hall doorway. No longer wearing his dark glasses, he stared at her with the coldest sapphire-blue eyes she'd ever seen.

Dressed in black, he held some kind of hand gun aimed at her.

Chapter Eleven

"What do you think you're doing?"

His words hit like ice pellets as he advanced into the room, slowly lowering the weapon to his side.

"You...you're not blind," she stammered. Reality seemed to have deserted her, had left her essence floating crazily in space.

"And you're not Dani Breckenreid." He held the gun in his right hand, cradling it in his left. He didn't take his piercing, blue-eyed assessment from her face. "So let's get down to some basic honesty, shall we?"

"No!"

She lunged for the back door. Aladdin's roar filled her ears as the big dog landed between her shoulders. The last thing she remembered was Andrew's yell to halt and toppling headfirst into the kitchen table.

****

When she returned to consciousness, she lay on the parlor sofa, a cold cloth on her forehead. Andrew sat on a footstool beside her. She stared up at him, for a moment not remembering what had occurred, barely recognizing him without his dark glasses.

"Sorry about what happened." He wet his lips. "Aladdin's been trained to react to anything he sees as a threat to me. He leaped at you before I could stop him. He has hair-trigger responses."

The word "trigger" brought everything tumbling

back. The gun in his hands. His not being blind. Lies. Deceptions. She had to get away from it all before it devoured what was left of her sanity.

"Don't," he said.

"What?"

"Try to make another run for it."

Oh, God, now he was mind reading.

"Or you'll do what? Lock me in that God-awful bathroom of yours? Or maybe you've got something even more hideous in the basement of this mausoleum."

She looked up at him dressed in black pants, shirt, and leather jacket, his gaze so intense it seemed to cut straight through to her soul, and wondered if she'd ever really known this man.

"You're being irrational, and you know it." He ran his fingertips down her left cheek, sending a thrill coursing through her. "Lie still. We have to talk."

"What can there possibly be to discuss? You deceived me, made a fool of me…"

"Not deliberately. I'd already established my blind persona before you arrived on the island. Actually, that's not true. It had been established for me."

"You've lied so much you can't even figure out the truth!" She put a hand to her forehead and groaned. It hurt. She wasn't surprised, considering the size of the egg rising there.

"I'll tell you why I did what I did, if you'll lie still and listen."

"Oh, good, another story." Courage fueled by anger burst into flame. "Does this include the reason for the gun, about your not being blind…"

"Dani, please listen." Something about his expression softened her outrage.

"Talk." She looked up at him with what she hoped was a hard, cold stare. "But I'm not agreeing to believe you."

"Fair enough. Here it is. I'm working with the RCMP. The blindness was part of their plan." He leaned back, away from her, but remained seated on the stool beside the couch. "They figured no one would pay any attention to a blind, lame man struggling to come to terms with his disability alone on a deserted island. That way I'd be safe until the trial."

"How do I know you're telling the truth...this time? You've pretended to be blind, you've..."

"I know, I know. I'm hardly someone you'd believe."

"Andrew, I don't know what to believe." She heaved a sigh. "You've told so many different stories..."

"Andy. Call me Andy. That's what my friends and family used to call me...when I was allowed friends and family. Andrew is that phony blind guy hiding behind sunglasses."

"Andy, I..." She reached out to stroke his jaw, but he lurched away.

"Don't." He stood and went to stare out the window at the still waters of the bay, where a thick fog bank was gliding toward shore. "We can't get involved. We've both got far too much excess baggage."

"Then what?" She peeled back the quilt and got up slowly, testing her balance. Her head throbbed as she made her way to his side.

"Dani...ah, damn!"

He caught her in his arms and kissed her with such passion shock waves of desire skyrocketed through every vein in her body. Broad shoulders, powerful chest, and hard belly pressed against her, leaving no doubt of the intensity of his emotions.

"I have to leave Phantom Island," he muttered against her hair finally. "That's what I found out when I supposedly went to the doctor's. I was ordered to break it off with you and never contact you again."

"But why?" She looked up into his face suddenly taut and hard. "After the trial, after those people are behind bars…"

"Believe me, this isn't what I want." He stilled her protests with a finger placed gently on her lips. "But there's no other solution. I don't want to put you in danger."

As he started to move away, she felt the lump on the left side of his chest and realized it was the gun in a holster.

"You're wearing a weapon."

"Yes." He paused in the foyer beside a packsack and a camera bag.

"And you're leaving…now?" The words came out in a burst of incredulity. "Right now?"

"I was upstairs packing when Aladdin and I heard you come in." He checked a fastening before hefting the packsack and camera bag onto his shoulder. "I thought it was someone coming to get me. Right now, there's a boat waiting. We have to leave while the fog offers cover. Goodbye, Danielle."

Without looking back, he strode out the front door, Aladdin at his heels.

What was happening? He wasn't blind, he'd kissed her like she'd never been kissed… She stood stunned with shock.

No, no, no! I won't let him leave like this!

Coming back to mobility, she ran out of the house and down the ragged steps to the beach. A thick, murky fog had moved in, making it impossible for her to see more than a few feet in front of her.

She arrived on the shore in time to see Andrew in silhouette throw his luggage into a waiting dory. Another man, also dressed in black, was at the oars. The outline of a dog—Aladdin, she presumed—sat alert and watchful in the prow.

Andrew gave the skiff a quick, powerful shove out toward deeper water, then leaped aboard. His companion put his strength to the oars, and the boat shot off into the fog.

"Andy!" she cried, running across the shore and into the shallows, but the dory, propelled by a strong oarsman, disappeared into the cloying mist. Her world crumbling in the miserable October morning, she let the icy water swamp over her feet, its bitter cold wafting all the way to her heart.

Suddenly she remembered. He'd called her Danielle.

****

Andy Drack sat in the dory's stern, cold to the bone, colder than even the foggy October day warranted. He wanted to tell his friend to turn the boat around, to take him back. He wanted out of the entire situation. But that couldn't happen. He knew it all too well.

"She's innocent, you know," he said. "They framed her."

"You haven't found any proof of it. In fact, most of the evidence points in the opposite direction. Her relationship with Hank Rockenfeller alone is enough, never mind those artifacts under the false bottom in the trunk of her car."

"Damn it, left alone, I would have been able to exonerate her. She trusted me. She even accepted the idea of that surveillance stuff I was using, that I inadvertently may have let her see in the closet when I hung up her jacket, being legitimate photography equipment from my fake former profession. A smooth operator like Hank Rockenfeller would never work with someone as naïve as Danielle Burgess."

"Your Dani did phony up a new name and profession to avoid coming forward in the museum heist."

"I told you. She's a severe claustrophobic. I saw irrefutable evidence of the fact. It's my guess the idea of incarceration would be enough to drive her to panic and run away. She's different from any other woman I've met on the job. She's caring and decent and vulnerable."

"So are you, buddy." The man at the oars didn't miss a stroke.

"Caring and decent, I hope, but vulnerable? In this line of work? How long do you think I'd last if I were?"

"I'm not saying you've been that way very long." His companion paused and rested the oars on the gunwales. They were completely engulfed in fog and their voices had an eerie quality in the silence. "I only saw it starting after you met this girl, as you got to know her."

"Are you accusing me of losing it?" The words shot out, hot and defensive.

"No, just of being, like the song says, 'lonely too

long.' Look, Andy, maybe it's time you gave some thought to giving it up, getting out of this particular area of work. You've given it ten years. That's more than most men could take. How long has it been since you've seen your family or had a real date with a woman?"

"Come on, pal." Andy hunched forward. "All I said is I believe Danielle Burgess is innocent. I don't need a lecture on family ties or my sex life. You can tell my folks I'm fine and that I love them all."

"Your mother would like to hear you say that in person." He took up the oars again and gave a pull.

"Haven't you been letting her know that I'm safe and sound?" Andy Drack looked sharply at his companion. "I trusted you to take care of it."

"Of course I have. I only said she'd like to hear it from you next time. Your dad is concerned, as well. And Chantale would like her boys to get to know their legendary uncle before they're ready to go off to college."

"Guilt trips don't work with me, and you know it. My family understands what I do and why I'm doing it. Someone has to. I will admit the adrenaline rush I used to get at this point in a case has been dwindling lately. Now let's drop the whole subject. It's starting to get to me, and I can't afford to be distracted...not today, and definitely not tonight."

"Okay, okay." His companion pulled harder on the left oar to turn the boat in the opposite direction. "Just wanted you to know I'll be around if you need to talk."

"Appreciate it."

The sleek white cruiser loomed out of the fog in front of them. Andy Drack climbed its side and vaulted over the railing onto its deck.

"Wait for him," one of the men on the ship instructed the oarsman. "We'll be sending him back to the island within the hour."

Chapter Twelve

"Miss Breckenreid?"

When Danielle heard the knock on her back door, she'd leaped from her chair to answer it, feverishly hoping Andy had recanted his resolve and come back to her. Now she couldn't decide if she were more appalled or disappointed by the presence of the RCMP officer in denim shirt, jeans, and black leather jacket.

"Yes, of course." She held the door open to allow Constable Wade James to enter. *Not in uniform. Does that mean he's not here in an official capacity, that he doesn't plan to question me, to arrest me?*

After Andy left her on the beach and sailed off into the mist, she'd been convinced her life couldn't possibly get any darker. Looking at the Mountie and visualizing a prison cell, she knew it could.

"Please...sit down." She struggled to keep the shakiness out of her voice as she indicated a chair at the kitchen table. "Would you like coffee? I made a fresh pot."

"Thank you kindly," he said, rubbing his hands together as he sat down. "I came over in Jimmy's old lobster boat, and the wind over the water cuts to the bone."

"I take it there's a compelling reason for this visit?" She handed him a steaming mug and sat down opposite him with hers, trying to control the shaking in her hands.

He was a strikingly handsome man: tall, broad-shouldered, brown-eyed and dark-haired, with a face now compassionate and kindly but which she had no doubt could be hard as stone when the occasion warranted.

"I came to talk to you about something I consider vitally important." He raised his cup and took a sip, watching her over the rim.

"Vitally important? What do you mean?" Her heart became a hard, cold lump.

"Miss Burgess...Danielle, I know who you really are."

"What are you talking about? My name is Dani Breckenreid." Tingling with terror, she tried to reply with utter surprise. "I'm a photographer from Ottawa..."

"There's no point in denying it. I've got a picture." He pulled a leaflet from his pocket and spread it out on the table. Her photo. And below it, "Danielle Burgess, archivist sought in theft of Egyptian artifacts from Eastern Coast Museum."

She felt the blood drain from her face. Words wouldn't come.

"I wondered about a young woman who would rent a cottage on Phantom Island in October on the weak excuse of photographing a ghost ship that hasn't been seen in years," he said. "So I did some checking. Later, when those artifacts were discovered under the false bottom in the trunk of your car, I was convinced your purpose in being here was far from innocent."

"False bottom in...? What are you talking about?"

"A major collection of small but extremely

valuable Egyptian artifacts were discovered hidden in the trunk of your car."

"How? When? By whom?" Lightheaded, Danielle could barely coordinate her thoughts sufficiently to ask.

"Not important. The fact remains that they were."

"Am I under arrest?" Nausea roiled in her stomach. She didn't dare to stand, in case her legs deserted her.

"No." He stood and went to top up his coffee. "Not if you choose to cooperate."

"Cooperate? How?"

"Help us to catch the major players in this scam."

"I don't see how I can."

"I'm beginning to agree with Andy." He leaned back against the counter and narrowed his eyes. "I think Hank Rockenfeller and the good doctor pulled you into their scheme without your having the slightest idea what they were up to."

"Hank Rockenfeller? The good doctor? Who are you talking about?"

"Hank Rockenfeller is known to you as Dr. Harry Stone. Hank is a major art thief. He killed the real Dr. Harry Stone in Cairo the day the artifacts were shipped to your museum, stole his papers and identity, and took his place on the flight to Canada. The good doctor to whom I'm referring is the man you know as Dr. Gervais Harrison. He's an international art facilitator, of the criminal variety, who has gone under a series of aliases, his most recent being this Harrison identity. He learns what country or individual wants a particular work of art, and he goes about securing it for them."

"No, no, you have to be wrong! I know Dr. Stone and Dr. Harrison... They couldn't possibly be..." And suddenly she recalled telling the sympathetic Dr.

Harrison about her claustrophobia.

Oh, God! By revealing myself as terrified of being confined, I made myself the perfect patsy. He had every reason to believe I'd bolt rather than face incarceration. And if Dr. Harrison and Harry...Hank... whatever...are in league...

"Miss Burgess, how many art thieves do you know personally?"

Again, the shrewd, narrow-eyed gaze.

"None that I was aware of."

She lowered her head to stare down at her hands. *Has the whole world gone crazy...or fallen apart, or what? You have to focus. He's speaking again.*

"Miss Burgess, Andy didn't believe you were involved, in spite of evidence to the contrary, and he's been proven in the past to be an excellent judge of character. I'm going to take a huge leap of faith and go along with him regarding you. You can prove your innocence by helping to catch the perpetrators."

"And why would you take Andrew Drack's word?"

"He's been my trusted friend for years. Now, are you willing to assist?"

"How?"

"By continuing to live here, by continuing to appear to be hiding from the law. Our informants tell us our suspects plan to bring the remainder of those artifacts, the ones you've been suspected of stealing, here tonight to deliver them to foreign buyers waiting in a vessel off shore. If you're not on site as they expect, it could scare them off. My colleagues have put too much time and effort into setting up this operation to have it go belly up now."

"You're trusting me not to try to warn them?"

"My superiors will be convinced of your innocence and your dependability if you agree to assist us, for several reasons." Brown eyes focused on her. "First, your past history is impeccable. Secondly, we've been monitoring your CB and you've made no attempt to send a message to anyone. Thirdly, a man with an excellent track record for instinct and integrity is willing to stake his future on your innocence. |And fourth, you've got virtually no choice beyond a jail cell. I understand you'd be quite adverse to the latter."

"Andrew…Andy?" In an instant her blood was racing at triple speed. "He's the person who vouched for me. You took him away last night, didn't you. You were the man rowing the dory! You know where he's gone…"

"I didn't offer the name of your reference. We're both acquainted with Jimmy Waters."

"You weren't referring to Jimmy Waters," she cried. "Don't play games with me, Constable."

"I'm definitely not playing games, Miss Burgess." Again deadly serious eyes locked her attention. "The name of our mutual friend doesn't matter. All I need is your guarantee of cooperation."

She paused, then drew a long, exasperated sigh.

"There's no choice, is there?"

"Not really."

"Then you'd better fill me in on what I'm to do." She leaned back in her chair, feeling empty and desolate in spite of the Mountie's offer of a chance to redeem herself. She could see he wasn't going to tell her anything that would help her find Andy.

"Okay," he said. "Here's the story. *Objets d'art* are being taken out of Canada and sold either to wealthy patrons eager to see these items returned to their homelands or to wealthy individuals so anxious to have them in their own very private collections they're not especially concerned about how the pieces have been acquired. To get sufficient proof to take into a law court, we have to catch the perpetrators actually delivering the stolen merchandise to the middle men in the deal. That's where you come in. We think those artifacts are going to be transferred to foreign agents waiting aboard a ship not far from Phantom Island."

"Why here? With all the miles of coastline…"

"Because of the island's unsavory reputation for ghosts, shipwrecks, and the like, it's generally avoided by locals. More importantly, and unlike most waterfront properties, it hasn't yet been discovered by tourists or people hoping to build vacation homes."

"You said this is where I come in." She looked over at him. "What do you expect me to do?"

"I believe you want to clear your name once and for all?"

"Of course."

"Then you won't object to helping us in this operation we have planned for Halloween."

"That's tonight!" Danielle gasped.

"Correct. According to our sources, the thieves will arrive here tonight to meet their overseas buyers, who'll be coming in to Phantom Island by motor launch from a larger vessel waiting offshore."

"Surely they don't believe I'll go along with their plan?"

"No." He looked squarely at her. "Do you know the meaning of 'scapegoat'?"

She gasped. "You think they plan to leave me to

take the blame?"

"Haven't they already?"

"But surely they don't think I'll sit idly by and…"

"You'd have to be silenced. These are ruthless people."

"What you're saying is I have to work with the police. It's my only chance."

"Pretty much. For what it's worth, I don't believe you're in any way involved with these people."

"I recall your reasons." *Trapped, trapped. I have no choice…beyond a jail cell, that is, and I couldn't bear that.* "Nevertheless, I get the feeling you think that even if I'm not directly involved with criminals, I'm a dubious character."

"You did use an alias, change your appearance, and falsify your reason for coming to the island." He looked at her so piercingly she wanted to squirm like a guilty child. "Only Andy's feeling so certain of your innocence swayed me. I had a difficult job convincing him to take you camera shopping and to lunch while I searched your cottage. Then there was that tanker accident and I couldn't manage it. We both decided he had to get you away again to allow me a second opportunity."

"You searched my house?" Heat flooded her face as she realized he must have found those oh-so-sexy bits and pieces of clothing.

That lovely lunch and romantic dinner had all been a ruse. Damn, how could I ever have thought I was falling for such a deceiving…

"It's my job." He shrugged. "When I failed to find anything, he supplied a wineglass with your fingerprints so they could be run through the computer and prove you had no priors. I'm sorry, but it was necessary. We had a warrant."

"Oh, I'm sure it was all very legal!" Pain and mortification metamorphosed into outright rage.

"Yes, it was." He appeared undeterred by her anger. "The difficult part was convincing Andy to go along with the plan and keep you out of the way while I conducted the search."

"Why should he have cared at that point? It's obvious he was acting as your agent."

"Simple." Constable Wade James met her confused, troubled gaze head on. "The man did something he should never have done, something which can't be allowed to continue. He became emotionally involved with a suspect, a person who could have proven deadly dangerous to himself and others."

A wave of joy washed over her, even as "can't be allowed to continue" echoed in her ears. Andy did care. He had trusted her.

"Are you saying Andrew—Andy—is one of you?"

"He's been an undercover agent for nearly ten years, but after this... Our superiors don't tolerate one of our people getting involved with any civilian who is part of an investigation, least of all a person of interest where crime is involved."

"What will be his fate for so dastardly a deed?" Sarcasm colored her retort. "Will he get a good dressing down about the evils of becoming friends with women in the course of his work?"

"No." Again the even, unemotionally professional tone. "Disenfranchising him from the source of his weakness should be enough, given his past record."

"Meaning me."

"Precisely."

"Well, that's the end of it, isn't it. Now suppose you tell me what I'm to do." Danielle struggled to appear casual as she fought off the twin sensations of being both trapped and emotionally crushed. To think she'd been falling for an undercover agent, someone who could change his persona as easily as a chameleon changed color.

"Keep on here as you are, pretending you know nothing of their plans. We'll be in the vicinity to make certain no harm comes to you."

"I'm sure you will be." She hesitated. "It's just that...I'm no hero. Probably that's why I was chosen to be their fall guy."

"Then it's time you proved them wrong," he said. "If it's any consolation, I think you're underestimating yourself. Any woman who'd come to live alone on Phantom Island and brave its beaches alone at night isn't a coward. I'd say you suffer more from trusting the wrong people than from cowardice."

Her entire world was turning upside down. She grabbed her cup and took a long drink in an effort to steady her swirling senses.

"You're right. I did trust all the wrong people." She looked over at the Mountie.

"You're not alone. Believe me." He stood, gave her a reassuring smile, and headed for the door. "Don't feel duped. These people are hardened professionals. They've fooled clever people all over the world."

"Wait! Will you at least let Andrew—Andy—know I'm going to be okay? We are...were friends. I'm sure he's concerned."

"Who?" He turned back to her, his hand on the

doorknob.

"Oh, I see." She didn't try to disguise the anger and exasperation his reply inspired. "He's ceased to exist, has he?"

"I'm sorry." His brown eyes softened with compassion. "You've been living alone here too long with yarns and legends as your only companions. Take my word for it, you'll be much happier once you accept the fact that Andrew Drack was simply a product of your imagination."

"Don't try to make me sound like a mental case."

"I didn't mean to imply that you were suffering from any such illness. Please, just take my advice and forget the name Andrew Drack. He doesn't exist and never did."

He went out, shutting the door after him with a definite firmness.

She wrapped her arms about her and shivered in spite of the fire warming the cottage from the living room hearth. She wanted to see her parents and her brother. She wanted to tell them she loved them and hear them respond likewise. She wanted to stop being alone and lonely. And most of all, she wanted the excruciating pain to go away. The pain of missing a man who had never really existed.

Bibsy, as if sensing her friend's unhappiness, leaped onto her lap, looked up into her face with wide, yellow eyes, and meowed softly.

"Thanks." Danielle cradled the little cat in her arms. "I need all the love and support I can get just now."

Chapter Thirteen

The day seemed interminable. Danielle cleaned the cottage and tried to read a photography book. It only served to remind her of another photographer, bogus though he'd been. By late afternoon she was pacing the length of the living room.

"This time tomorrow it will all be over," she told Bibsy, who sat watching her from the comfort of the couch by the fire.

The little cat glanced over at her and made a squeaky feline sound.

"You're right," she said. "I should take Constable James's advice and forget Andrew Drack. But this waiting for night, for whatever that brings... I have to do something, or I'll go mad." She drew a deep breath. "So I'm going to look for the horseman. I know I saw him. That manure on the lane to Andy's farmhouse confirmed it. Since I already know he doesn't keep his horse in Andy's barn, there's only one other place left on this island to search."

****

Twenty minutes later, at the fork in the road, she took the turn to the old cannery. The day was still, cold, and gray. There'd been heavy frost in the night, which slightly warmer morning temperatures had turned liquid. Now it dripped in icy droplets from brown fern fronds, ragged grasses, and scraggly dark branches.

With a shiver she drew the hood of Hettie Matthew's jacket over her damp hair and trudged into the overgrown trail, rubber boots flopping on her feet. She was glad she'd left Bibsy in the cottage. This definitely wasn't a day for hedonistic felines to be abroad.

Just when she was beginning to wonder if there was any cannery at the end of the trail, or indeed any end to it at all, she emerged into a clearing where a group of sagging shingled buildings was strung out in the tangled weeds and grasses just above the beach sand.

A ghost of an industry. The thought flashed through Danielle's mind as she paused to peruse the forlorn scene. Once this place must have buzzed with activity, a business had flourished, people had made a living. Now it was a rotting ruin left to the caprices of wind and weather for its final demise.

Enough fanciful thinking. She'd come to find a horse. After scanning the clearing to reassure herself that she was alone, she moved out into the open, toward the least dilapidated of the buildings, the only one that seemed barnlike enough to serve as a stable, with a door large enough to admit a horse.

As she moved closer, she watched the ground for any indications that a horse had passed that way. She found no hoof prints, but the battered weeds and recent rains could have hidden them. Moreover, an animal could have been brought to the shed from any direction.

A few feet from its entrance, she halted. Her breath caught in her throat. The sandy ground had been mangled by horseshoes!

She crept to the door and lifted the wooden bar that held it closed. With cold perspiration trickling over her body, she eased it open a crack and peered into the dark interior. A snort, a soft whinny, and restlessly stamping hooves made her freeze.

Again the soft whinny. It came from the far end of the building and sounded almost welcoming. When no human response followed, she eased inside and paused to allow her eyes to become accustomed to the gloom.

At first she could see little, but as her vision adjusted to the shadows, she discerned the outline of a horse's head thrust over the boards of a box stall at the far end of the building. Bales of hay were stacked along a nearby wall, a pitchfork and a water bucket beside them.

The horse whickered again and stretched his head toward her. Cautiously she walked toward the animal and saw his breath puffing out in foggy gusts in the cold air as he pranced, excited by her approach.

"Hello, boy," she spoke softly. He snorted and shook his head. He was very big and very black, but he seemed friendly as he strained toward her, ears pricked.

"Are you the phantom's horse?" She moved close enough to reach out a cautious hand to pat his thick, arched neck. He muttered softly and nuzzled her jacket pocket.

"So the phantom brings you treats. He must be a caring kind of ghost."

Her eyes now fully accustomed to the barn's shadowy interior, she saw a stock saddle resting on a sawhorse in a corner. A bridle and reins hung on a peg above it, a bag of grain on the floor beneath it. A shelf to the left held a box of brushes and other grooming equipment. A pair of binoculars lay on top of the pile.

"You've been well provided for," she said,

wandering over to pick up the binoculars. "How often does he come to care for you? Morning and evening? More importantly, who is he? Where is he now?"

She put the binoculars to her eyes. And gasped. Night vision apparatuses. There could be only one reason for the phantom horseman to have such sophisticated equipment. He was a sentry, watching Andy even at night, riding the beaches, spying on him, planning the best moment to close in for the kill!

She dropped the glasses back in place, turned, and fled, barely pausing long enough to close the door behind her. She had to get back to the cottage and radio Wade James on the CB.

****

Running, slipping on slimy weeds and grasses, stumbling over roots, Danielle sprinted back to the cottage through the woods. Evening was fast approaching, and she had no desire to be out alone in the darkness. It would have been shorter to go along the beach, but she couldn't risk being seen.

She had a painful stitch in her side by the time she burst into the field behind the cottage and skidded to a halt. In the twilight, lights shone from its windows. Someone was inside. There were no vehicles besides her old car in the yard. Andy? It had to be! He'd come back to her, probably in the same boat that had taken him away.

She began to run again, her heart beating wildly, this time with joy.

****

"Danielle! I've been waiting for you. I came out by boat a half hour ago and couldn't think where you'd gotten to. God knows the night life on this scrap of flotsam must be limited."

For a moment Danielle thought she was dreaming as Harry Stone got up from a chair at the kitchen table and came to take her in his arms.

Shocked, she could only stand robot-still. Thoughts tumbled over one another in her astounded mind. Harry Stone, alias Hank Rockenfeller, whom Wade James had declared an art forger and a murderer.

Her stomach roiled as she realized the full extent of Harry Stone's deception. The man had made her believe he was her only chance of salvation, but all the time he had been setting her up to take the blame for his crime. Enraged, Danielle thought for a moment that if she'd had Andy's gun at her disposal she could have shot him for all the hours of fear and outright terror he'd forced her to endure. Then she remembered her promise to assist Wade James and his colleagues.

"Harry, what a wonderful surprise!" With a gargantuan effort she forced herself to appear glad to see him. "Have you solved the mystery? Are the perpetrators in custody?"

"Everything is coming to a satisfactory conclusion…soon. Join me." Harry released her and took a bottle from an ice bucket on the counter. "We're celebrating, girl!"

"Celebrating?" Danielle removed her wet jacket, hung it on a peg behind the kitchen door, and bent to remove the rubber boots. "Celebrating what? Am I free to leave this awful island?"

Oh, God, I'm not good at role playing, at deception. Please, please don't let him suspect…

"Celebrating the successful conclusion of the case of the missing Egyptian artifacts."

"You've found the thief?" Danielle padded barefoot into the living room and paused, astonished. "Who was it?"

"A guy named Grant Casey." Carrying the bottle and two glasses, he followed her and plopped down on the sofa. "He's internationally known as an art thief. He takes orders for art collectors wanting certain pieces and countries eager to repatriate pieces of their history they considered stolen or confiscated."

"Grant Casey?" Danielle was amazed at the ease with which the man she'd known as Harry Stone was able to lie. "I've read about him. I understood he stuck to big museums with vast collections. I find it difficult to believe he'd bother to come all the way to Nova Scotia for a few Egyptian artifacts. There are so many others in collections all over the world."

"Ah, but not so easily accessible." He poured wine into both glasses. "You have to admit, Danielle, the security system at your little museum is hopelessly outdated. Or maybe he just decided to visit the area." Harry shrugged. "He's a world traveler. He may even have had an order for those particular pieces."

"Did they apprehend him?" Danielle pretended she was completely captivated by the story. Her heart raced, half from fear, half from excitement. The game, as Sherlock Holmes would have said, was most definitely afoot.

"Grant Casey?" Harry's laugh was harsh. "Can you capture the wind? Believe me, he's just as elusive."

"How did you discover he's responsible for this particular theft?" Danielle began to push paper, kindling, and wood into the fireplace, hoping he wouldn't notice the trembling that afflicted her hands.

"So many questions." Harry laughed again, but this time Danielle heard a ring of the ruthlessness in it. "I'll explain it all later. Put a match to that pile, will you? This place is freezing. Then come and have some wine."

Kneeling on the stone hearth to do his bidding, Danielle glanced at the bottle and at Harry, who'd poured out a generous glass for her, and determined she wouldn't drink a single drop.

"There." She stood to watch the flames beginning to leap in the fireplace. "It'll be warm shortly. I'm going to change out of these wet clothes. Make yourself at home. I'll be back in a minute. I want to hear all the details of the great Egyptian robbery and how you solved it."

Alone in her bedroom as she changed into another sweatshirt, another pair of socks, and her running shoes, she formulated a plan to escape and warn Wade James. Risky and far from foolproof, it was the best one she could come up with.

"Much better," she announced brightly, returning to the living room. "Nothing like dry clothes to make a person feel better. Now how about that wine and the story?"

"Definitely." Harry handed her the already filled glass with such alacrity she guessed it was drugged, possibly to the lethal point. Scapegoats had to be disposed of.

His fingers touched hers on the cold surface, and she had to struggle not to flinch away. *Reptilian. How could I ever have found this man attractive?*

"To our future." Harry raised his glass and touched it to Danielle's. He watched as she raised the wine to her mouth. She closed her lips and hoped that no liquid would pass them.

"Ummm." She lowered her glass and smiled. "This is good. But I'd better not have too much. I have a low tolerance for alcohol."

"Not to worry, my sweet." Harry bent close to her. "I'm here to take care of you now."

"Speaking of low tolerance"—Danielle turned toward the kitchen, glass in hand—"I have to feed my cat. If any creature ever had a low tolerance, it's Bibsy for hunger. I'll be right back."

She cast him a smile over her shoulder as she headed for the kitchen. Once out of his field of vision, she sneaked to the sink and poured three-quarters of the wine down the drain. Then, making as much noise in the operation as possible, she opened a can of tuna for Bibsy, who sat atop the refrigerator. She scraped it noisily out into the cat's bowl and clattered it onto the floor. Finally, with her heart racing at breakneck speed, she eased her way toward the back door.

In the living room she glimpsed Harry Stone peering out the window into the fog.

Turning away, she lifted Hettie's jacket from its peg.

"Going somewhere?" He stood in the kitchen doorway. He must have moved as quickly and silently as a cat. He was smiling, but Danielle had seen friendlier displays of teeth in *Jaws*.

"Thought I'd check the generator's fuel supply while I'm up and about," she tried to sound cheerful and casual. "I wouldn't want to risk a blackout while I have a guest."

"Never fear," he said, advancing slowly toward

her, still smiling. "I took the liberty when I arrived. Everything in the shed is as it should be."

He's searched the place! He wanted to make sure I'm alone!

"Terrific." She moved away from the door and picked up her nearly empty glass from the counter. "I'm really not feeling much like going outdoors again tonight." She turned to him and tried for what she hoped was a tipsy smile.

"Come on, let's go into the living room and enjoy the fire." He took her arm and guided her into the adjoining room and onto the couch.

"You're really a very nice man, Harry." She slurred her words, hiccupped and forced what she hoped was a foolish grin across her face. "I wish…"

She let her words trail off as she slouched against him, the glass toppling from her fingers.

"Danielle?" He shook her gently.

She mumbled and imagined herself a rag doll.

He stood and let her slide, face down, into the cushions.

"You can come in now," he said. The front door opened. "She's out like a light."

Danielle heard something being placed on the coffee table and fought the urge to rub a cat hair from her nose.

"What an incredible pushover," Harry muttered against a background of rustling sounds she assumed were made by packing materials being pushed into place. "She's the most gullible creature I've ever met. She never once questioned that newscast about her being the prime suspect in the theft, never once suspected it came from a CD I slid into the car's player while she was in that service station washroom. For sure she never once suspected her absentminded boss, Dr. Gervais Harrison, of being one of us. It was a stroke of genius for him to fake a heart attack after he got the security codes to me and have himself hospitalized at the time of the heist, leaving his archivist to take the blame."

"You said there was no security guard. Hard to believe, with such a valuable collection involved."

"Small museum, tight budget. They had to be content with the local RCMP making a check a couple of times a night. Easy pickings, given how easily this cookie here on the couch was to finesse into taking the blame."

Danielle hoped the flush she felt rising up her cheeks at his words wouldn't be noticed. *Damn Harry Stone or whoever he was! And a major Egyptian curse on the creature who'd called himself Dr. Gervais Harrison.*

"Moving fast must have been a major factor," the unknown voice chuckled. "If you'd given her time to come to her senses, face the situation calmly and rationally, I doubt your scheme would have worked."

"Well, I didn't." Harry Stone's reply smacked of such smugness Danielle longed to leap to her feet and fly into his face like an enraged Bibsy. "The thought of incarceration panicked her. Claustrophobia proved a powerful tool to use against her. Sending her into hiding out here with these goodies stashed in the trunk of that wreck of a car was my particular stroke of genius. All it took was a few romantic dinners and she trusted me completely."

"Trusting people are the easiest to use," his

companion replied.

I want to kill him, to kill them all. Outrage knotted in her stomach; her heart hammered.

"Stop prattling! They're coming…"

Danielle heard the soft purr of a powerful motor as some sort of craft came to shore, then footsteps on the veranda. The front door opened and shut again. New characters had entered the scenario.

"Come in, my friends!" She heard Harry Stone greet the newcomers with alacrity. "See what I've brought for you, hidden under the floor of the trunk of the old car I got for her. And there's more in the boat on the beach."

Packing material rustled.

"Magnificent!" declared a soft voice with a foreign accent that reminded Danielle of every Dracula film she'd ever seen. Footsteps advanced toward the coffee table.

"As promised." Harry Stone's voice was triumphant. "I can get you anything you want, out of any museum in Canada. The good so-called Dr. Harrison is a great partner. He can inveigle his way into a position of trust anywhere. He and I are a dream team. Now, as to payment…"

"Not yet, my friend," a second, thickly-accented voice cautioned. "You made a serious mistake. You must right it before we will consider the assignment complete."

"Mistake? How? I've covered every detail, right down to producing a scapegoat."

"You overlooked the blind man in the farmhouse." The cold, smooth voice sent a chill over Danielle.

"Blind man? There's no one…"

"Ah, but you're wrong. There's a man living in that old house. He claims to be blind. We don't believe it. Burn the house, and make sure he's in it. Afterwards, set this excuse for a cottage ablaze. We want no habitable dwellings left on this island. We will use it as a pickup point again."

"I didn't see anyone at the farmhouse when I arrived this afternoon." Harry Stone was clearly eager to end the business. "You're wrong."

"Ah, but we did. Just now we saw a lens glinting through the fog. When we sent in a scout, he discovered the not-so-blind man and his dog. Now go. You'll find a can of gasoline on the beach."

Andrew was back on the island? She had to warn him that these people were plotting his murder!

"Okay, okay," Harry snapped. Footsteps headed for the door before it slammed.

There were several moments of silence, then the dreadful voice of death continued, "When he comes back, get rid of him…with this cottage and the girl."

"Understood. He's been sloppy, much too careless to be of any further use."

"Too bad," the first voice said. "The girl on the couch…she's a pretty thing. She might have been a pleasant diversion on the voyage home. Nevertheless, not worth the trouble she might cause. Come along. We've merchandise to load."

The door opened and slammed shut again. Danielle heard footsteps crossing the veranda, then silence. For what seemed like hours she continued to lie perfectly still. Finally she slowly opened first one eye, then the other.

The room appeared deserted. From what she could

see through the windows, in the fog and darkness, the veranda was also empty. Her heart banging so furiously she was sure it was audible, she slithered to the floor and across the room. Casting frequent, furtive glances over her shoulder, she crawled into the kitchen.

Once there, she scrambled across the floor and lifted the rug-covered hatch. Managing to hold the piece of carpet in a position to recover the opening, she dropped into the black hole beneath.

The moment the hatch shut after her and dank, murky blackness surrounded her, panic seized her. Something cold and wet slithered around her ankles and up her legs. Stuffing a fist into her mouth, she suppressed a cry.

Water. That's what it was. Water that must have flooded the small basement during the storm. She couldn't stay in that awful place, she couldn't…breathe. Her head swam, and terror gripped every inch of her being. She had to get out!

Andrew's words came back to her, describing how fear for the life of his father had forced him to overcome his phobia and board that plane. She had to do the same for him.

Footsteps sounded, crossing the veranda, entering the living room.

"The girl! Where is she?"

Something that sounded like a curse in a foreign language followed. She listened to footsteps pounding about the cottage, at one point directly over her head. Finally they stopped.

"This is not a time to go rushing madly about," the second foreign voice commented. "She can't get off this island. We'll find her. Make sure Rockenfeller does as instructed. I want that spy in the farmhouse burned to ashes."

"Of course."

"I'll come with you. We'll look for the girl along the way. She must have gotten outside."

Hurried footsteps marked a departure. Danielle swallowed hard and drew a deep breath. She could do it. She had to. No matter how Andrew—Andy—Drack had deceived her, she couldn't allow him to be murdered.

She waited for what seemed an eternity. At last, convinced by the silence above that the cottage was deserted, she decided to make her move.

Shaking so violently she could barely coordinate her movements, she eased the hatch open a crack and surveyed the kitchen. Empty. She crept up the steps and out onto the kitchen floor.

Drawing a deep breath, she bolted to her feet and sprinted out the back door into the darkness and the long, dead grass behind the cottage. *I have to warn Andy. I have to.* The words chanted inside her head as she ran toward the cover of the forest of black spruce.

"There she goes! Stop her!"

"Argh! Cat! Get this creature from hell off of me!"

A roar, a feline shriek, and a shot.

Oh, God, no! They've shot Bibsy! She dodged and zigzagged through the fog on legs that didn't seem to belong to her body.

A second bullet plowed into the sand inches from her feet, spewing stinging fountains of sand up her legs.

Hoof beats. Racing toward her. She skidded to a halt as a horse and rider emerged from the trees mere feet in front of her.

A gunman behind her, the phantom horseman galloping directly toward her, Danielle Burgess was trapped.

Chapter Fourteen

Bent low in the saddle, the horseman burst out of the fog and headed toward her. This time he wasn't wearing his cloak, mask, or hat. Danielle stood rooted in place as he bore down on her.

He looks like… No, it couldn't be.

A split second later, a strong arm snatched her up and she was half dragged, half flung up onto the horse. The pommel struck her ribs, and she yelped in pain.

"Hang on! For God's sake, hang on!" Above the thunder of hooves and rush of air, Andrew Drack's voice hammered out the order.

He whirled the horse as another bullet ploughed into the sand between the animal's hooves. They raced off into the long grass toward the trees standing out bottomless and weird above scarves of low-lying fog. Danielle thought her insides would split, but knowing this was her only chance she clung to the saddle. Another bullet slammed into a spruce beside them as they gained the cover of the woods.

Once among the trees, Andy reined to a halt and let her slide to the ground.

"Get up behind me." He held down a hand as he kicked his foot from the stirrup in front of her. The horse pranced and blew as she staggered back a step, away from its cavorting hooves.

"Andrew…" His name was a gasp.

Andrew Drack is the horseman.

"Get up! No questions." He bent down to seize her shoulder in an iron grip, the planes of his face hard and grim.

Another bullet whizzed through the branches above her head. With a *yike*, she grabbed his hand, put her foot in the stirrup, and vaulted up behind him.

"Put your arms around me and hang on," he ordered. He made a kissing sound to the horse and they were off in a lunge that all but unseated her. She grasped his body in a desperate grip.

Her thoughts were a tangle that held no answers, but that didn't matter. She and Andrew Drack would probably die in a hail of bullets in this mad dash through the fog and darkness.

Trees slapped at them before they burst into a clearing. Andy reined the horse to a prancing, plunging halt. Above the noise of stamping hooves and blowing nostrils, Danielle heard shouts to halt, shots ringing out, and a confusion of men's voices and orders being yelled somewhere in the mist behind them.

"It's over, Andy," Wade James' voice informed them over a loud hailer. "Come on in."

Andrew Drack touched his heels to the horse. It broke into an easy trot toward the sound.

"Andy, why...who...what?" she tried to ask against his black leather jacket.

"Later," he muttered.

They arrived on the beach as the fog began to lift. Peering over her companion's shoulder, Danielle saw two men in handcuffs surrounded by a black-dressed group holding weapons.

"Great! You got 'em!" Andrew Drack reined the

horse to a halt. "What about the ship offshore?"

"Got that, too," one of the black-clad figures turned toward them, and Danielle recognized Constable Wade James. "Our marine division was ready and waiting. The only one we're missing is Rockenfeller."

"He went to burn the farmhouse," Danielle informed him. "They"—she pointed to the captives— "thought Andrew...Andy would be inside."

"Aladdin still is!" In a single motion, Andy Drack whirled the horse about, all but unseating her. "I left him guarding the surveillance cameras. Danielle, get down."

"No." She tightened her grip. "I'm going with you. I want to be in on that bastard's capture."

"Let go!" Andrew tried to shake her loose but, being behind him, she had the advantage.

"Andy, look!" Wade gestured toward the house. Flames shot out of an upstairs window.

"Sweet Jesus!" Andrew swung his horse around. "All right, Miss Danielle Burgess, you're coming along."

He yelled to the horse, causing it to leap forward. Danielle felt her bottom momentarily leave the animal's rump, then return with a hurtful thump that knocked the breath from her body. She didn't care. She was on her way to capture that miserable piece of trash Harry Stone, or whatever his real name was.

As Andy urged the horse up the slope into the front yard, Danielle lost her battle to stay aboard and slid over the animal's flanks to the ground.

"Are you okay?" He pulled the cavorting horse about and looked down at her as she stumbled to her feet.

"I'm fine. Hurry! Get Aladdin!"

He whirled the horse back toward the house, yelling and kicking his heels against its sides to send it racing toward the structure. At the front steps, he leaped to the ground and sprinted toward the door.

Before he could reach it, a figure darted out of the dancing shadows at the rear of the house and made a dash for the woods.

Above the roar of the flames, a great snarl erupted. Aladdin burst through the kitchen window. In a flash he'd crossed the yard and brought the fleeing figure to the ground with a mighty leap.

"Help me!" the man yelled as he fell face down on the ground, the snarling dog on his back.

"Aladdin, halt!" Andrew Drack, a drawn gun in his hand, ran forward to order the dog aside. "Danielle, come on! We have to get out of here fast. The house is about to collapse."

Together they forced Harry Stone a safe distance from the fire. Andrew pulled a pair of handcuffs from his belt and secured him to a tree.

"Danielle, I never meant..." The man she'd known as Dr. Harry Stone stumbled out the words. "You and I have a good thing going..."

"Oh, I'm sure you thought we did." She glared at him. *Giving me one last try. Incredible.* "Now I can only hope you rot in hell!" Her hand shot out and landed a resounding slap across his face.

"Good." In the lashing shadows of the flames, Andrew Drack grinned down at her. "You had to get that out of your system." He whistled, and the big black horse that had raced away when his rider leaped from its back came trotting up to him out of the dissipating mist.

"I have to go." He caught up the animal's reins and turned to Danielle. "Wade and the other officers will be here shortly to pick up the prisoner."

In the darkness, the leaping flames of the burning house behind him, Andrew Drack was an incredibly virile, incredibly mysterious, totally irresistible figure. Every nerve, every sensation in her body rushed to fever pitch. The excitement of the past few minutes had left her supercharged.

She put her arms about his neck and pulled his head down to kiss him with a wild, fiery passion she'd never known she possessed.

****

He knew he should get away. Fast. But his body had other plans. As her mouth covered his, he abandoned rules and regulations and crushed her to him. Every curve of her body molded into his as if it had been made to order.

What the hell. He'd earned a few minutes alone with her before he left. He relaxed and indulged himself in her wild sweetness and the sincerity of her desire for him. An urge to carry her off to some secluded place and spend the rest of the night making love to her engulfed him.

He knew from previous experiences that it was partly the aftermath of dodging bullets, but this was something more. He couldn't afford to start thinking that way.

"Andy, where are you? Are you okay?"

Wade James' voice brought him back to reality.

"I'm fine. I'll be right with you, Wade." He pulled away and looked at her. "Danielle, I've got to go." He hurt as he saw the confusion her eager face reflected. "I don't really exist. You've got to understand. There is no Andrew Drack. There never was."

"Just like the character in *Frenchman's Creek*," she murmured.

"Damn!" He cut off her words as he kissed her again, suddenly, fiercely. His arms became steel bands binding her to his hard, thoroughly aroused body.

"Know that you're one very special lady," he muttered hoarsely against her hair when he finally released her lips. His chest was heaving, his words shaking with emotion. He released her and, before she could find words of reply, swung back onto his horse. "Then, forget you ever met me, and get on with your life...Dona."

"Andy!" Wade James' voice sliced through the smoke.

"Coming." He whirled the horse about, and, after a final look at the woman he'd left standing in shock, galloped off up the beach to disappear into the darkness and tattered fog. His wolf dog bounded after him.

She leaned against a tree as a dry, deep pain stabbed into her chest. Harry Stone had betrayed her, Bibsy was dead, and Andrew was gone...forever. She couldn't cry. Some hurts were too deep for tears.

Chapter Fifteen

Stumbling in the darkness, she started back toward the cottage, where searchlights and flashing police beacons brightened the surrounding night. The stabbing pain in her chest made her gasp as she walked, but she had to get back, to find Bibsy...Bibsy whose bravery had given her the few precious moments she needed to escape. She choked as her last meal threatened to return. Gulping, she made it into the circle of light and organized confusion surrounding her home.

Three boats were leaving the shore, filled with men dressed in black and the others, shackled, who she assumed were the ones who'd come to her cottage to meet Harry Stone...Hank Rockenfeller...his fellow criminals. Far out on the water, the lights of two larger boats, side by side, indicated the presence of more police and the capture of the criminals' vessel. One boat remained as two officers headed up the shore to collect the man handcuffed to the tree.

Wade James stood alone on the beach, a solitary figure in black, holding the horse's reins. She went to join him, her chest still heaving.

"Miss Burgess." He turned to her, and she saw the effects the tense evening had had on him mirrored in his face.

"Constable." She looked up at him. "So it's over...finally over."

"Yes, quite a Halloween." His mouth quirked into a sardonic grin.

Is this how these men view such an experience? With a kind of wry sense of humor? Maybe it's the only way they can manage to continue to do this kind of work.

A whine close behind her made her start. Whirling, she saw Aladdin. An overwhelming sensation of joy wafted over her. Aladdin was still here. That meant Andrew...

"Aladdin will be staying with me." Constable James killed her hope. "As is Cavalier." He rubbed the horse's neck.

Aladdin poked at her hand, and she stifled the urge to shove the dog away. Misery was making her unkind.

"He wants something." Wade James looked down at the dog. "He wants you to follow him."

Bibsy. He's found Bibsy's body. I have to go and retrieve it. I have to give her a decent burial.

"Aladdin, seek back." The Mountie gave the order, and the dog bounded into the darkness near the back doorstep of the cottage. With her companion leading the horse beside her, Danielle followed.

Please, please let her have died instantly. Please don't let her have suffered.

In the illumination of the constable's flashlight, in the weeds under the back door step they found the small body. Blood covered her shoulder, and she wasn't moving. Aladdin dropped down beside the little cat and whined.

Oh, Bibsy! Danielle fell to her knees and put a hand to the soft fur. A shock raced through her. The cat's side was moving, slightly, but moving.

"Constable, I think she's alive." She looked up at the officer. He knelt beside her and ran his hands over the small animal, pausing beneath her front paws.

"You're right. Alive, but just barely."

"She saved my life! She delayed them long enough that I could get away. We have to do something for her."

The constable paused a moment, then turned his head to speak into the radio on his shoulder.

A half hour later a helicopter whirled to a landing in the field behind the cottage.

A medic jumped to the ground and ran toward the couple. "Where is the patient? Gunshot wound, I understand?"

"Here." Constable Wade James extended the blanket-wrapped bundle with the small, unconscious cat's head visible.

"A cat? You ordered a copter medic team for a cat?"

"This cat is a hero." He handed Bibsy over to the astounded man. "She saved a human life tonight. The least we can do is try to save hers."

"Okay." He took the bundle. "But there will be hell to pay for this, Constable. I hope you're ready to live with the consequences."

"Definitely. Now you'd better get on your way. Oh, and Miss Burgess will be accompanying you. It was her life Bibsy saved."

"Bibsy? Oh, why not. Come on, miss. I'll do my best, but we'd better get her to a vet asap."

He started back toward the helicopter, ducking under the whirling blades.

"Thank you." Danielle looked up at Wade, hoping

the sincerity and depth of her gratitude appeared in her eyes and face.

"All part of the job." He touched his forehead in salute. "Now go. I don't know how long those guys will be patient."

She rose on tiptoes and planted a quick kiss on his cheek before running off toward the waiting air ambulance.

As the helicopter rose into the air, she looked down and saw him in dark silhouette, the horse and dog by his side as he stood alone on the beach. The Horseman of Halloween, she thought fancifully, remembering the date before turning her attention back to the medic working over Bibsy.

****

With Bibsy declared out of danger by the vet in New Harbor, Danielle returned to Phantom Island the following day to pick up her personal items from the cottage. She'd spent the night, or what was left of it after Bibsy's successful surgery, at a nearby bed and breakfast, thanks to a credit card provided by a member of the New Harbor RCMP. Constable Wade James met her on the shore as she disembarked from Jimmy's ferry, driving a similarly funded rental car. Hers had been seized as evidence. He was mounted on the black horse she'd ridden with Andrew.

"Out for a canter?"

"Just a final gallop before I take Cavalier back to the mainland." He grinned.

"I'm surprised you're still here."

"Final maneuvers." He quieted the restless horse. "Although we're ninety-nine percent certain we got all the bad guys using the island, my superiors wanted me to stay out here a while longer to be sure we got everyone and everything before we close up shop."

"Shop?"

"Our investigation required one of our members to ride the beaches at night disguised as the horseman."

"Why not an ATV?"

"Two reasons. First, an ATV makes noise, needs lights to find its way, and leaves tracks difficult to eradicate. Second, a man in black riding a dark horse can be mistaken for a shadow or perhaps even a figment of the imagination. We needed someone on the island to play the part and keep a constant surveillance. We needed someone who was an excellent horseman as well as a good actor. Andy Dumont met those requirements."

"Andy Dumont?" The word "actor" sent a wave of nasty distaste washing over her.

"Otherwise known to you as the mysterious, dark stranger Andrew Drack." He quirked an eyebrow and a corner of his mouth. "The lame blind man who couldn't possibly see anything, nor ride a horse, not with a crippled leg."

"So Andy Dumont is an actor?"

"Among other things. He's one of our best undercover agents. Like a human chameleon, he can turn himself into a lot of different personas."

"And Jimmy… He's one of your people, as well?" She glanced back to where the old man was bustling about his ragtag ferry. He'd promised to wait while she got her belongings and to return her to the mainland.

"Not officially, but he has been keeping an eye on comings and goings around here for us." He looked at the ferryman and smiled. "Great old guy, Jimmy."

"That's all I need to know. I'll get on to the cottage and gather up my things. The sky has that grayish-white look it gets just before it snows. We wouldn't want to be caught out here in a snowstorm." She started to put up her window, but the man on the horse stopped her.

"The little cat. How is she?"

"Going to be all right, thanks to you and that helicopter crew." She paused. "What will happen as a result?"

"You mean to me?" He shrugged and adjusted the regulation RCMP cap on his head. "A good dressing down, a couple of weeks' suspension without pay, probably nothing worse. Fortunately, our inspector is a feline fancier. He understood what I did and why."

"And Aladdin, what about him? Where is he? What will become of him if there's no actual Andrew Drack to take care of him?"

"He'll be provided for."

"And the horse, Cavalier?"

"He's destined to go back to the RCMP stables in Ottawa. He'll be given another assignment."

"So Andrew...Andy Dumont wasn't his owner, his exclusive rider?"

"No, otherwise do you think I'd be sitting this comfortably on his back?" He patted the animal's arched neck and was rewarded with a snort. "He's one powerful fellow and could throw me halfway across this island if he chose. Being accepted by Cavalier made it possible for me to take a turn now and then at playing the horseman. You'll remember you saw him when you were with Andy that first night you spent on the island."

"How did you manage to get the

horse…Cavalier…out to the island in the spring without anyone noticing? A horse trailer on Jimmy Waters' old ferry would have attracted attention."

"No horse trailer." He patted the horse's arched neck. "I led him aboard in the middle of the night and held him quiet for the crossing. Jimmy took a big risk, ferrying us out here without using lights on his old rig." He paused to look up at the sky. "We'd better be going. As you say, there's a storm brewing, and we'd best not be caught out on the water aboard Jimmy's less-than-stellar craft."

"Wait!" She stopped him as he started to turn the horse away. "What…what about the person you call Andy Dumont? Where is he? Where will he go next? I know he's not supposed to exist, but we both know he does."

"I honestly can't tell you." Constable Wade James held the impatient stallion to a pawing stance. "No one but the top brass knows where he'll be sent next. His identities and his location have to be top secret. Sorry, Miss Burgess—Danielle—but you'll have to forget you ever met him. It's for the best."

Chapter Sixteen

"Put the star on the top, Danielle."

Matthew Burgess handed the ornament to his daughter. "I know Barry usually does it, but he won't be here for a while yet, and we want to finish trimming the tree before dinner."

"You're being kind," she said softly. "Really, Dad, you don't have to pamper me. The people who tried to make me look like a thief are in jail, and"—she took the star and climbed up the stepladder—"there really was a man named Andrew Drack, no matter what the RCMP and that old scoundrel Jimmy Waters said." She placed the ornament atop the bushy fir and turned to her father. "Okay?"

"Okay." He understood the double meaning. "Whatever you say, honey. And the star's fine, too."

"Matt, Danielle, come and help me get dinner on the table. It's nearly six. Barret will be here shortly. I want everything to be ready...especially since he's bringing a friend."

Ellen Burgess appeared in the archway, a trim figure in a soft pink turtleneck and gray pants partially covered by an apron adorned with a holly sprig design.

"Your wish is my command, my darling." Her tall, white-haired husband snapped to a mock attention and saluted. "Let us, as they say, hop to it, my child." He extended a hand to Danielle and ceremoniously helped her climb down.

"Mom, I hope this man Barry is bringing home for Christmas really is a friend of his and not another of your attempts at matchmaking." Danielle followed her slender, blonde mother into a kitchen fragrant with roasting turkey and laden with pies, breads, vegetables, and stuffing.

Bibsy, curled up on a cushion in a corner, greeted her with a meow, eyes bright and unblinking as she waited for her Christmas dinner. The little cat had recovered fully and received a hero's welcome into Danielle's parents' home every time they visited from her mistress's apartment.

"Danielle, I'm hurt." Ellen took a steaming pot of potatoes from the stove and poured them into a colander at the sink. "You'd think I was some kind of conniving mother who's desperate to see her daughter as happily married as herself."

"Why don't you pick on Barry?" Danielle began to rip up lettuce for the salad. "Why not marry him off? He's older than me."

"Who'd have him, with his lifestyle—a day here, a week there, a month somewhere else? No, my darling, you're the designated one, always dependable, always..."

"Gullible, easily panicked," Danielle finished bitterly and sliced into a cucumber with more vehemence than necessary. "Those are the characteristics that got me into trouble, remember?"

"We're home!" a familiar male voice called out as the front door opened. "Make us welcome."

"Barry!" Danielle snapped back to the moment. Drying her hands on a tea towel, she turned and rushed into the foyer. Once there, she stopped so quickly she nearly toppled headlong.

A man stood beside her tall, handsome brother, an equally tall, equally handsome man in a RCMP uniform, a silver wolf dog by his side.

"Hello, Danielle." The officer removed his fur hat and smiled.

"Andrew?" Suddenly lightheaded, barely recognizing him, she stared.

"Andy Dumont," Barret said, his expression anxious. "Sergeant Andrew Dumont, actually. I told him this wasn't a good idea. You're white as a ghost, little sister. I told him he ought to ease into this."

"Andrew Dumont?" Danielle was still reeling from surprise. "You really are French?"

"Half. French father, English mother, remember? Thus my name. One of the few things I told you that was true." He grinned sheepishly.

"All part of your job, as I understand it." The initial surprise past, resentment billowed up. "Like leaving me standing alone in the fog, like making me sound like a crazy person who'd invented you."

"I'm sorry about all that. I wasn't proud of what I had to do. So I've come to tell you the truth, Dona." He hesitated, apologetic. "I couldn't go on trying to let you think you'd imagined me, like my superiors ordered. Aladdin..." He turned to the dog. "It's Dani, the lady who saved your life. Go and thank her."

The big dog's tail had been wagging gently since he'd entered the house. Now, released from restrictions, he bounded to Danielle and leaped up to try to lick her face, all but knocking her down.

"Enough already!" Andy called as Danielle

laughingly managed to withstand the dog's gratitude. "Back to heel," he told the dog, and then to Danielle, "I'm sorry for all you've been through because of my undercover activities." Blue eyes sincere, he looked at her as Aladdin obeyed. "I had to come to see you now because it's well and truly over. I'm back on regular uniform duty. All that's left of those times is Aladdin. He's become my own dog." He patted the animal and self-consciously avoided her eyes.

Sergeant Andrew Dumont, who'd braved bullets and smugglers and living alone in an eerie old mansion that would have made Dracula apprehensive, was shy and ill at ease as he apologized to her. In that moment he was irresistibly appealing and she could forgive him anything.

"Let me take your coat and hat, Sergeant." Matthew Burgess and his wife had come from the kitchen and were greeting the man with their typical alacrity. "It's not every Christmas we have a will o' the wisp to dinner."

"I thank you kindly, sir." Andrew Dumont kept his gaze on Danielle as he spoke. "I don't plan to stay. I only came to explain to Danielle."

"Nonsense, man," Matthew started to continue. "There's plenty of food and…"

"Dad, I think Andy and Danielle need a few minutes alone." Barret Burgess had removed his captain's cap and coat and was herding his parents back into the kitchen. "Danielle, take Andy into the living room. I'll keep these two busy."

"Come in." She indicated the big living room to the left.

"Thank you kindly." Repeating himself, he

reflected his unease. He stamped snow from his boots on the doormat and followed her into the room lighted by a fire crackling on a stone hearth and the Christmas tree twinkling with lights in the bay window. Aladdin wandered, sniffing, toward the kitchen.

"Danielle, I'm truly sorry for the distress I caused you." His gaze searched her face for her reaction. "Sometimes catching the bad guys exacts an unfair toll on the innocent. Unfortunately, sometimes there's no other way."

"If you hadn't carried the operation through to its conclusion, I would never have been cleared of those charges. In fact, I probably wouldn't even have survived," she said softly, toying with a tree ornament. "There's nothing to apologize for. But I'm glad you chose to come here to explain, where my parents and brother can see you and know I hadn't..." She stopped short and turned to look out the window into the darkness and softly falling snow.

"Hadn't imagined me?"

"Yes." She swung back to him, her heart racing. *This is ridiculous. We're acting like two bashful teenagers.* "Andy, I'm so glad you've come."

"Really?"

"Really."

"Good. Well, then, good." He turned to gaze into the fire. "All the way to Egypt I couldn't concentrate, thinking about how I'd left you. I couldn't leave things between us like that."

"Egypt? You've been to Egypt? Why?"

"I had to tie up some loose ends on the art robberies," he said. "Hank Rockenfeller murdered the real Dr. Harry Stone and stole his papers shortly before the flight that was to carry him and those artifacts from Cairo to Canada. He resembled Dr. Harry Stone in a general sort of way, and since no one in this country had ever met the real archeologist, he was able to carry out the hoax. Among the doctor's papers was Harry's great-aunt Hester's will. The placement of that cottage fitted right in with what Hank needed as a rendezvous point for meeting with his foreign buyers."

"You had to go to Cairo to gather evidence?"

"Exactly. I called Wade to ask him to check up on you and make sure you were okay. He told me how you'd managed to elude those killers in the cottage and make that desperate attempt to escape to warn me."

"I couldn't let them kill you," she murmured. "We were…friends. And as the horseman, you saved Bibsy and me the night of the hurricane."

"Friends. Right."

"That was quite a trick, you and Wade James taking turns to play horseman so I wouldn't suspect you."

"We've worked well together ever since our days in University. We planned our strategy when we learned from Jimmy that you were coming to the island. Wade was supposed to search your cottage the day we went camera shopping and to lunch. Unfortunately the tanker accident kept him engaged, so I arranged for us to have dinner that night."

"He told me about his search. Go on, tell me the rest." Wanting to get away from the subject that reminded her that the officer must have seen her sexy clothing, Danielle struggled to suppress the blush flooding up her face.

"On the return flight from Egypt, I discovered our

captain was Barret Burgess," he continued. "I'm not a man who believes in signs or omens, but a coincidence like that couldn't be denied. So here I am."

"So, from the beginning, you conspired to get close to me so you could keep an eye on me and learn if I really was a criminal." She cocked her head to one side and narrowed her eyes. "What I've been left wondering is just how far you would have gone to get information from me. How long were you supposed to keep me entertained that night Wade James was searching my cottage?"

"As long as I could." He looked gently down at her. "Unfortunately, I lost my objectivity that night. The day you drove me to my supposed doctor's appointment, I had a meeting with my CO. I asked to be allowed to trust you, but his answer was a definite no."

"That's why you were so irritable during the drive home. That's why you said we couldn't see each other anymore."

"That's right," he said. "I knew I had to vanish once the case was concluded, that I wouldn't be allowed to materialize on that island ever again. So I did as instructed. But when I met Barret on my return flight from Egypt, I knew I had to give us another chance. I went to my superiors and explained the situation. After a lot of arguing, they gave me permission to see you again and explain. They also advised me that if that was my decision, my days undercover could be over."

"You've lost your position with the RCMP? Oh, Andy, I'm sorry!"

"Note I said 'could.' I think they'll come around. Getting involved with you was the first time I've ever let myself get personally entangled with a suspect."

"So I *was* a suspect?"

"Very much so…especially after the horseman discovered those Egyptian artifacts hidden under the fake floor of your car's trunk. Hank Rockenfeller must have secreted them in that old car sometime before you parted company with him. It was a good way to get them transported to the coast, have them out of his possession—not that he thought he would get caught, but just in case—and make you the scapegoat if you happened to get caught."

"They were in that old car?"

"Hidden under a false floor in the trunk. The horseman found them shortly after you arrived on the island."

"No wonder you suspected me. I'm amazed you didn't arrest me right then and there."

"We were out to catch the whole gang." His mouth quirked at one corner. "You, Danielle Burgess, were considered only a minor functionary in their operation."

"Minor functionary! As if… Ha!"

Her outburst was stifled as he reached out to take her into his arms.

"Think there's any future for us?" he asked against her hair. "I have this crazy lifestyle…"

"I know, I know." She looked up at him and felt a smile tugging at her lips. "But, maybe, just maybe, I'll be willing to give it a try."

"Well, then, good, very good." He lowered his head to kiss her but stopped as her father entered the room.

"Dinner's waiting, you two. We'll give you time for smooching afterwards. Right now, food's cooling."

"Smells great." Andy grinned as Danielle took his hand to lead him to the kitchen, then paused.

"But the sighting we had of the Fire Ship…was that just another part of your sting operation?"

"Definitely not. I saw it, too. I thought it possibly was something you and your fellow conspirator Dr. Harry Stone had set up as a signal of sorts. That's why I got so riled when you missed getting a photo of it."

"But it wasn't…was it?"

"No. Guess we were granted one of those rare viewings."

"Maybe it was a sign…a sign of all the romance and mystery that was ahead of us." She slanted him a coy smile.

"Maybe."

"Just a few more questions before we go in to dinner. Why did you call me Dona when you left me that night on the island…and again when you came in just now?"

"A du Maurier fan like you has to ask?" He was grinning, the blue eyes she loved twinkling down at her. "Dona was the woman who shared all those wild adventures with the mystical Frenchman in *Frenchman's Creek*, don't you remember?"

"Of course!" Delight filled her words. "You thought…think…I'm comparable to her?"

"Better." He looked down at her, teasing now. "You're not married. I don't have to send you back to your husband and kids."

"I found a photo of the horseman in the pocket of Hester Matthews' jacket. Can you explain that?"

"I think she must have caught me during one of my practice rides when I first came to the island."

"She never found out it was a real flesh-and-blood creature she saw?"

"Not to my knowledge. Maybe it was just as well. The poor woman spent so many years trying to capture a photo of a ghost, and just before she died, she believed she'd succeeded."

"Hurry up, you two." Her father's voice brooked no further dallying.

Another thought hit her.

"Oh, my God! Bibsy! Aladdin went into the kitchen, didn't he?"

"Yes, but…"

"Bibsy can't jump up on things nearly so well since she was shot! He'll…"

"I don't think you have any need for concern." He stopped as she made a bolt for the kitchen. "Wade told me it was Aladdin who found Bibsy after she was shot. I think I can safely say that action declared a truce between them."

"Well, let's hope you're right."

"Come on, you two! Dinner's wasting." It was her father again.

Danielle shrugged and grinned up at Andy. "Think you can put up with this kind of pressure?"

"I'm willing to give it a serious attempt." He gave her a quick kiss before they headed into the kitchen.

When they stepped into the room redolent with the smells of Christmas dinner, both stopped abruptly, astonished.

"What do you think of that? Is it an omen or what?" Matthew Burgess gestured toward a handhooked rug by the rocking chair where Aladdin lay, Bibsy sitting between the big dog's front paws, contentedly grooming herself.

"Looks as if the future is off to a great start." Danielle squeezed Andrew's hand.

"And well it should be. It's not every day a phantom and a fugitive get together, never mind a pair of sworn enemies like that cat and dog."

A word about the author...

Gail MacMillan is the award-winning author of over thirty-three published books, with numerous articles published in magazines throughout North America and Western Europe.

Visit her at:

macgail@nbnet.nb.ca

~*~

Other Books by Gail MacMillan available from The Wild Rose Press, Inc.

Non-Fiction:
How My Heart Finds Christmas
To All the Dogs I've Loved Before

Historical Romance:
Highland Harry
Heather for a Highlander
Shadows of Love
Caledonian Privateer
Lady and the Beast

Contemporary Romance:
Cowboy and the Crusader
Counterfeit Cowboy
Rogue's Revenge
Holding Off for a Hero
Ghost of Winters Past

Thank you for purchasing
this publication of The Wild Rose Press, Inc.

If you enjoyed the story, we would appreciate your
letting others know by leaving a review.

For other wonderful stories,
please visit our on-line bookstore at
www.thewildrosepress.com.

For questions or more information
contact us at
info@thewildrosepress.com.

The Wild Rose Press, Inc.
www.thewildrosepress.com

Stay current with The Wild Rose Press, Inc.

Like us on Facebook

https://www.facebook.com/TheWildRosePress

And Follow us on Twitter
https://twitter.com/WildRosePress